T0208552

GOLDEN AGE
Dating

ELIAN HEN-NINVE

BALBOA
PRESS
A DIVISION OF HAY HOUSE

Balboa Press books may be ordered through booksellers or by contacting:

Balboa Press
A Division of Hay House
1663 Liberty Drive
Bloomington, IN 47403
www.balboapress.com
1 (877) 407-4847

Because of the dynamic nature of the Internet, any web addresses or links contained in this book may have changed since publication and may no longer be valid. The views expressed in this work are solely those of the author and do not necessarily reflect the views of the publisher, and the publisher hereby disclaims any responsibility for them.

The author of this book does not dispense medical advice or prescribe the use of any technique as a form of treatment for physical, emotional, or medical problems without the advice of a physician, either directly or indirectly. The intent of the author is only to offer information of a general nature to help you in your quest for emotional and spiritual well-being. In the event you use any of the information in this book for yourself, which is your constitutional right, the author and the publisher assume no responsibility for your actions.

Any people depicted in stock imagery provided by Getty Images are models, and such images are being used for illustrative purposes only. Certain stock imagery © Getty Images.

Print information available on the last page.

ISBN: 978-1-9822-0624-6 (sc)
ISBN: 978-1-9822-0623-9 (hc)
ISBN: 978-1-9822-0625-3 (e)

Library of Congress Control Number: 2018906816

Balboa Press rev. date: 06/07/2018

Reading Pinkola Estes's book was, for me, a kind of an initiation ceremony, like receiving an invitation to participate in an ancient ritualistic ceremony in which all of the women of a tribe gather around bones and sing. The power of their singing fuels life into the bones.

In that place, in that sacred moment, at night, we connect with our feminine roots. Singing around the bones gathered by the old woman La Loba connects us, in the author's words, to our female infinite cycles of the moon; the seasons; and the cycles of life, death, and life. We channel into the life system within us, connecting to one another and to all of nature.

From within the pages, I can hear her say to me, "You are a woman, and I am a woman. I know how hard it is for you to live in our patriarchal world, realize your freedom as a woman, and express yourself as who you are. I wish to remind you through these stories and to connect you to these primal ancient places hidden in you, in us, from which you can derive strength and faith. These are the dark circles of female power and strength: fertility and nature."

Clarissa Pinkola Estes calls us to trust our instincts, our inner strength, our nature, and the love within us. We must return to our roots embedded in nature and understand that we are not apart from nature, nor are we different from it. She is sending us to the wild parts with the old woman La Loba. Join her. Sing with her to the bones, which will fuel life into the dead bones. This is the prayer of all women, wherever they are, each and every one.

—Nava Telpaz, Jungian psychoanalyst
From the preface to the Hebrew version of *Women Who Run with Wolves* by Clarissa Pinkola Estes

Contents

CHAPTER

REY SAT IN FRONT of the TV, searching for something to watch. She found a show on the documentary channel about a sixty-year-old looking for love. "Okay," she said to herself, "let's see what this is about."

The program featured a divorced woman who'd decided to document her experience in looking for a loving relationship. Rey thought the program reflected a harsh reality. It showed a series of disappointing, embarrassing experiences that made it seem there was something pathetic in the attempt to find a loving relationship at that age. There was nothing positive about the experience. Rey felt angry and sad.

The next day, when she spoke with Batya, her spiritual mentor and best friend, she told her about the program and described her feelings at length. "You know," she said, "if I'd watch that show without knowing what I do and knowing that it can be different, I might have made an unbreakable vow to never get involved in the dating circle, in order not to expose myself to those experiences. Luckily, I know it can be different."

"True," answered Batya. "You experienced something entirely different."

"Indeed," said Rey. "There are disappointments, of course, and embarrassments, like in many situations at any age. That is part of the process. I can honestly say that for me, it was a unique, enriching experience. I have learned what is happening, what has changed in the interaction between men and women, and what is new. Most importantly, I learned about myself—not to mention all of the people I met on the way. Some are wonderful people, and some are not so much, but I can truly say I would not have passed on this opportunity."

"So why don't you write about it?" suggested Batya. "Write about your experience. Write a book, and call it *Golden Age Dating*."

"Wow," said Rey after a moment. "That's quite an idea. And the title hits the bull's-eye. Dating and the golden age seem to be unrelated subjects. True?"

"True," answered Batya. "Dates are bars, drinks, flirting, sex, and excitement."

"Good time for the young. The golden age, on the other hand, suggests nursing homes, doctors, medication, and geriatrics. But that's not necessarily true."

Ladies, I have news for you, Rey thought. *Buckle up. We are about to hit the road. It's a road to new horizons and new possibilities from a different angle, if you so wish. It's your call.*

The women of Rey's generation were expected to be modest, obedient, and virgins on their wedding night. Sex was something they never discussed, a word they could find only in dictionaries. They were curious and had questions but did not have anyone to ask. The girls grew up with bits and pieces of information that showed complete ignorance, such as the notions that boys had periods too and that when people made love, they lay on top of each other all night. That sounded uncomfortable.

Rey got married when she was nineteen after a boring and frustrating military service. She wanted to be trained and become an officer, but at the time, the higher-ups didn't consider women's wishes or qualifications, so she was sent to do clerical work in an army camp warehouse.

She wanted to be free and get away from her parents' responsibility. She loved Amiram, or at least she thought she did. She believed with all of her heart that getting married and having a husband would make up for all of the bad things that had happened to her, and her life would be filled with wine and roses like in the movies.

She was not a virgin on her wedding night, but Amiram was the one who had picked her cherry. Rey had no sexual experience and no idea how things worked in bed. The truth was, she was not particularly impressed with the whole thing. Given the choice between sex and a banana split, she preferred the latter. Amiram thought he was the ultimate lover and a maven when it came to women, and Rey had thought her first lovemaking would be like the description in Hemingway's book *For Whom the Bell Tolls*, when the woman felt the earth move, but the only thing she felt moving was Amiram.

It took her four years to realize that marriage was not what she'd expected. Amiram was tall and handsome, with beautiful green eyes and long lashes. He was the hunk in the band and a good guy. However, their life together, with his family in the same house and little privacy, was putting pressure on her and made her uncomfortable. She never had a key to the house, and her mother-in-law was possessive of her son, even hostile at times. After the wedding, she started looking for a job, and when she received her first paycheck, Amiram asked her to give him the money. He then gave her a monthly allowance for lunch and bus fare.

She was annoyed and angry.

Rey started looking for a way to get out of her premature marriage. She was not going to bury her life at the age of twenty-four. If she was unhappy, she would get up and leave. As of now, she was in charge of her life. She worked, and she earned a nice salary, meaning she was independent and needed no one's permission for anything. Her parents were horrified by her decision and didn't know how to handle it.

Rey's parents had divorced when she was six years old. When her father tried to convince her to stay with Amiram and talk her out of getting a divorce, she said to him, "You don't have a say in this matter. This is my life, and I know what is good for me. Besides, you got divorced from Mom, so how can you advise me on the subject?"

He answered, "I did not want to get divorced. It was your mother's wish. To be a divorced woman at the time was quite unpleasant due to the fact that men saw divorced women as secondhand goods—easy prey."

Rey didn't worry much about it. Fear of stigma was not a good reason to stay married. Besides, she would cross that bridge when she got to it.

Once she'd made up her mind, she left Amiram and moved in with a girlfriend. She took with her only a blanket, a pillow, a bed sheet, a couple of towels, and some personal stuff. She also got a farewell present from Amiram. He said, "You look hot, but the truth is, in bed, you are not worth much."

She felt tremendous relief. She was free to do as she pleased, and that was enough—for now.

CHAPTER

A YEAR AFTER SHE got her divorce, Rey met Mike and fell head over heels in love with him. The first time they made love, he said to her, "When I am with you, I think I've died and gone to heaven."

Amiram, did you hear that? Eat your heart out, she thought.

They broke up after six months. The timing was bad. Mike had just gotten divorced after ten years of marriage and two kids. He left everything to his wife just for the privilege of seeing the children at any time.

Rey was heartbroken. She thought maybe she could find a way to change his mind, but a year later, she realized that was not going to happen, and she gave up.

She decided to quit her job of seven years—at a place that was almost like home for her, especially since her divorce—and make a leap of faith into the unknown.

She got a job as an executive secretary in an oil field on the Sinai Peninsula. Everybody told her she was crazy, she shouldn't leave a steady job, the Sinai was the Wild West and not a place for her, and she was making a huge mistake. However, the opportunity was too tempting, and the salary was three times more than she was earning, so she packed a bag, went to Sde Dov Airport in Tel Aviv, and boarded a DC-9 army plane. On both sides of the aircraft were long, narrow seats. That type of army plane originally had been made for paratroopers.

Those were the days of the war of attrition in the Suez Canal. The passengers on the plane joked about watching for Egyptian MiG jet fighters. Rey was afraid of flying, even though she had flown before.

Sometime during the flight, the door of the cockpit opened, and a big guy wearing overalls, with a severe look on his face, came out and looked through the small windows.

"He is searching for Egyptian MiG jet fighters," whispered one of the passengers, who giggled.

"Who is he?" Rey asked.

"He is the pilot," the passenger said.

Rey felt cold sweat covering her body and thought, *If this is the pilot, who is flying the airplane? I must have been out of my mind when I decided to work in a place like this.*

After one hour, the aircraft landed on a strip in the desert, close to the beach but nothing else. The aircraft door opened, and a staircase was wheeled to the opening. The passengers started going down the steps as a gust of hot wind blew, and a flight attendant dressed in an orange miniskirt and a green shirt greeted them. She held the passenger list in one hand and her skirt in the other. She checked the names of the arriving passengers.

When Rey approached her, she asked, "Are you the field manager's new secretary?"

Rey said, "Yes. My name is Rey."

"Okay. I am Marina. You can come with me to the office. We will go have lunch, and then I shall introduce you to the boss, the oil field manager."

They got into a pickup truck at the side of the runway and rode together. The oil field looked like an army camp. The offices were a group of wooden buildings in a square shape. In the middle of the yard was a white cut-cement pillar. "Here was once a statue of Abdel Nasser," Marina said, referring to the former Egyptian president. They went into one of the offices, and Marina gave Rey a form to fill out. Then they walked to the camp dining room.

Rey could not figure out what she felt. The fear she'd felt earlier had been replaced by a feeling of awe at being in the desert, on the beach, and in the mountains, natural features from the beginning of time. The place had a primal quality. She was overwhelmed with excitement and on the verge of tears.

In the afternoon, she met her boss, the oilfield manager. He was a good-looking man about fifty years old and was pleasant. In his office, he explained the specifics of her duties as the oil field manager's secretary and his expectations of her. "Here we work ten days in a row, including weekends and holidays, and then you fly home and get five days off. On your days off, one of the other office girls will replace you, and you have to update each other to ensure the work order."

Rey's office looked pretty basic. It seemed not much had changed since the Egyptians occupied the place. The phones were for communication inside the oil field. There was also an SSB radio to communicate with the company's head office in Tel Aviv. On the wall were area maps and the oil field, along with photographs of the tank batteries and oil production charts. Everything was new, unfamiliar, fascinating, and somewhat

7

scary. The girls in the other offices told her they would love to show her the ropes.

During the afternoon, there was a lot of traffic along the office area. Zoe, one of the secretaries, came into Rey's office with a big smile. "Don't be alarmed," she said. "Word got out that the boss has a new secretary, so the guys are coming to check her out."

"What does that mean?" Rey asked.

"Nothing. Just play it cool. Stay busy working. Yes, they will try to come on to you, so prepare yourself for a romantic attack."

"To what do I owe the pleasure?" Rey asked.

"Well," Zoe said, "first, you are the boss's secretary, and also, there aren't too many girls around here. So enjoy."

At the end of the day, the girls took Rey to the living quarters: a big wooden cabin with four rooms, a communal shower and bathroom, and basic furniture like the kind she'd had when she was in the military service. Nothing was locked. This world seemed like a different planet and was exciting for her. It felt like a dream.

Between the girls' lodgings and the offices was an area of old, empty huts used during the Egyptian occupation for the oil field workers. The wind, which blew most hours of the day, caused the hut doors to open and shut, making scary squeaks that reminded her of Alfred Hitchcock movies. The squeaking sounded even scarier at night when Rey passed by on her way back from the office.

One morning, she decided to put an end to the sounds. She went from one hut to another, closing all of the doors. She made the mistake of telling the guys about it, and they kept teasing her, saying, "Don't worry, Rey; we'll find new ways to scare you."

Every day around three o'clock in the afternoon, the direction of the wind shifted, and a sea breeze started blowing. The smell of the salty sea air was intoxicating. Rey felt a sort of high most of the time. She needed only four to five hours of sleep at night, and she woke up in the morning feeling energized. Her coworkers told her it was the clean air.

That was the beginning of her romance with the desert. She'd never imagined that a place could awaken such strong feelings and continued awe. She remembered reading somewhere that the Sinai Desert was known for its strong, unique, powerful energies.

With time, Rey came to know the senior team of the oil field; the pilots; the ship captains who came down periodically to help navigate the oil tankers into the loading dock; the oil engineers; and all of the various experts, Israeli and foreign, who were part of the marine department crew. They were a group of ex-seamen—fascinating people who had many stories about adventures at sea, including hurricanes and rough seas. Rey listened eagerly, feeling envious.

There were also government officials and other VIP guests. Someone at the top always wanted to treat them and give them a tour of the oil field. One day Joe, one of the divers, came to the office and whispered in Rey's ear that the oil tanker captain was inviting her for dinner on board. Every now and then, when that Greek oil tanker arrived at the dock, the captain invited some of the marine crew and the divers for dinner on board. Rey looked at him, surprised. "He invited me? Why?"

"Rey," Joe said, "do you want to come, or do you want to keep asking silly questions?"

"Okay, okay, yes. Fine. Who else is coming? How—"

"We'll pick you up at seven," Joe said, and he left.

CHAPTER

REY HAD NEVER BEEN on board a tanker before. It was a fascinating evening. She was the only woman on board except for the captain's fiancée. Everybody spoke English except for the fiancée, a fat Greek lady who sat all evening and smiled politely. The captain didn't bother to introduce her to the guests, and since no one spoke Greek, she was silent most of the time. It seemed that what helped the woman not to scream in protest was a bottle of whiskey beside her, which was almost empty.

At the end of the evening, when the party was over, the captain gave Rey a bottle of retsina, a Greek wine with a unique taste. They all got off the tanker by the gangway and got on the adjacent tugboat, a small boat that maneuvered boats in and out of the marina.

Rey felt like Alice in Wonderland, and when she went home on vacation, she couldn't stop telling her experiences to everybody who was willing to listen—and those who were not. She told everyone about the wonders of her life in the Sinai.

Quite a few men tried their luck with her, but Rey decided to be cautious in her choices. It was a small place, and everybody knew everybody, including who slept with whom and when and where.

One of the men who courted her intensively was Avi, who was head of one of the departments. He wasn't her type and was married, but like most of the senior personnel in the oil field, he stayed there on his own; his family remained behind. The oil field was a kind of fools' paradise: one could live there as if the rest of the world did not exist. That was, in fact, part of its magic.

Rey was in close contact with Avi as part of her job, but it seemed to her that he visited her office more frequently than his job required. He did this gently and was not pushy, but he was consistent. She played it cool and was nice, as if not understanding his hints.

The divers who worked maintaining the underwater oil pipes caught big fish from time to time. On one of those occasions, they brought the spoils to the office and asked Rey if she would like to cook up something. Rey jumped at the opportunity to show off her cooking skills and decided to prepare something, especially since the girls had moved into the villa of one of the Italian oil engineers who'd lived there during the Egyptian occupation. It was a nice, spacious stone house with a big kitchen and a huge cooking stove. She decided to invite the divers, the girls, and a few other guests, including Avi.

It was a wonderful evening. The guys brought all kinds of goodies they took off of the tankers. The food was good, and there was a lot of booze. Everybody complimented Rey on the cooking, and whiskey was abundant. Rey drank moderately but felt great—free, even if somewhat tipsy. Finally, the party was over, and everybody left. However, Avi stayed.

Avi and Rey sat on the porch. The house was on the beach, and a pleasant breeze blew from the sea, bringing the wonderful, intoxicating, salty smell. There was magic in the air. Avi told her about his sea voyages throughout the world, the sense of freedom and power the sea gave him, the storms he'd experienced, the countries he'd visited, and his family. Rey told him a little about her life and about Mike. Finally, she said, "It's three o'clock in the morning, and tomorrow is a work day. We need a few hours' sleep to be able to function."

Avi thanked her again for the excellent meal and the pleasant company and left. Rey switched off the lights, entered her room, and went to bed. She couldn't fall asleep; she felt a kind of high from the whole evening. It had been something new, something she'd never experienced before. She was surrounded by different kinds of people—interesting people of the world—and they evoked in her a hidden sense of adventure and a passion to travel the world, discover new cultures, and meet new people. She also thought about Avi. She'd discovered a side of him she hadn't seen before. He was a real man and was sensitive, with qualities she had not encountered in a man before. Despite his tough appearance, he had manners and much respect and appreciation for women.

She barely woke up the next morning. She had a busy day ahead of her. High-profile guests from the head office in Tel Aviv were coming, which put a lot of stress on her boss, and he put stress on her. At ten o'clock, a wire from the corporate office informed them that the visit had been rescheduled. The new date had yet to be determined.

Rey entered her boss's office to give him the news. He pretended to be greatly disappointed, but Rey knew he was relieved, and so was she. The visit would happen another time. He stayed in his office, checking the new oil production reports. When he came out of his office, he gave them to Rey and said,

"Please add these figures to the chart. I want this chart to be updated daily."

He stood for another moment in front of the door and then said, "Rey, you know what we are going to do instead? I will give you a tour of the rig and the tank batteries. You have not been there yet, have you?"

"No," replied Rey, "I have not been there yet."

"Good. The helicopter pilot is ready anyway since he was supposed to fly the guests. I have not been there for a while. Tell him to be ready in fifteen minutes."

"Sure," Rey replied.

Rey had never flown in a helicopter before. They reached the landing strip and boarded the chopper. The rig was about ten kilometers from the shore, so it was a short flight. There was a marked landing spot on top of the oil rig for emergencies, such as in times of rough seas, when a supply boat could not approach, or when an evacuation was necessary. They landed, and the pilot remained on board with the engine running. He never turned off the engine because if there was a problem, there would be no way to remove the aircraft from there.

They went down a narrow, steep ladder. Since Rey was not prepared for this trip, she was wearing a short miniskirt. She looked down and saw the whole crew standing there with their heads up. She was embarrassed for a moment but then said to herself, *So what? I'm wearing a beautiful pink skirt with new white lace panties. Let them enjoy the view.* She confidently came down the ladder, and when she reached the bottom, she smiled and said, "Well, did you enjoy yourselves?"

The embarrassed guys burst into laughter and applauded her. "Good looking and cool," they said. That broke the ice, and she gained her place with the rig crew. The boss gave her a tour, explained how things worked there, and told her about the sea oil wells and the oil production. Rey asked many questions, especially about the tank batteries, where the oil was stored, and the jetty, where the oil tankers came over to load the crude oil. The boss was pleased to see his new secretary was so interested, and he explained things to her willingly.

Every day that passed, Rey was grateful for her choice to work in Sinai.

CHAPTER

AFTER THREE MONTHS, REY'S boss resigned, and someone else was due to replace him. The rumor was that Eli, the new boss, was a veteran and tough oil man. He summoned Rey to his office upon his arrival to the oil field. She entered his office and introduced herself.

"Hi. Pleased to meet you," she said.

"Likewise," he said. "I am Eli. Please have a seat. I have heard many good things about you." He smiled.

"Thank you," replied Rey.

"Okay," he said, "let's start. I do not want two secretaries. When I am here, you are here. I fly home every Thursday evening and return Sunday morning. You can do the same. I know that normally, workers here work ten days and then have five days off. If you choose not to fly home every week, that's up to you. Secondly, you have been here for three months now, so you are familiar with the routine and know the people involved in the daily operation of the oil field. You can do what you need to without asking me; you have my blessing. If you are not sure, ask me. If you make a decision that I think could have been done differently, I will tell you and explain why. You will never hear from me something like 'Why didn't you ask me first?' I think the best way to learn is with hands-on experience on the job."

Rey felt weakness in her knees at all of the responsibility. Now she'd have to give orders to those big machos with helmets. Suddenly, she realized Eli had a big smile on his face. "You look as if you have seen a ghost," he said. "From everything I've heard about you, I think once you get used to the idea, you'll be able to perform this job with flying colors."

"Thanks for the vote of confidence," replied Rey. "I will do my utmost to live up to these expectations."

It turned out that Eli was the best boss Rey had ever had. She learned to be independent, decisive, creative, and, most of all, authoritative. During the first department heads' meeting after his arrival, Eli said, "This is Rey, my secretary. I assume you all know her. You should view everything she says as if I have said it. If you have any comments or disagreements, you can tell me, but only after you've done what you were asked."

Rey felt a certain degree of discomfort, but she stayed calm, cool, collected, and professional. Eli lived up to his word, and she enjoyed working with him.

After the meeting, Avi came up to her and said, "Congratulations, girl. You should know that Eli's words, authority, and backup say a lot about your qualifications and professional abilities. If there was anyone here who doubted that, that's over now."

"Yes," she said, "that came as a complete surprise to me. I had no idea he was going to make such an announcement."

"So can I buy you dinner, and we can have a toast at the bedouin place?"

"Yes," replied Rey. "Definitely a reason to celebrate."

"Okay, I will pick you up at seven."

"Aye aye, sir," she said with a salute.

Rey and Avi became a couple. Rey wanted to keep that information private, but it was impossible in a small place like the oil field, so it became known that Rey and Avi were together now.

Rey discovered Avi to be charming, wise, sensitive, and considerate. He was a noble soul. She never heard him gossip or bad-mouth anyone, and she felt she was falling in love with him. Around him, she was at her best, and he caused her to be calm and relaxed. When they were together, she surrendered to those feelings for him, and she even told him, "I love you," with no fear or hesitation. It was odd since she was walking a dead-end road, but she enjoyed every moment, and the thought of where their relationship would lead never crossed her mind. During their time off, each went to his or her other life, real life. They never met or contacted each other. In the oil field, they were together, and that was perfectly okay.

People who worked in oil fields knew one another; they met over time in various oil fields and drilling sites at home and abroad, and they developed friendships and rivalries. Some of them met in the Suez oil field, and their disputes sometimes reached a state that did not enable a smooth and flowing work environment. Some of the disputes penetrated to the oil field and sucked much of the energy required to operate the field. Due to these struggles, Eli decided to leave his job as the oil field manager. Rey felt disappointment and sorrow. They had a great working relationship and a wonderful rapport. Eli did not have to tell her what to do; she always knew. When he first used to call her to his office to give her a list of things to do, he found out that most of the tasks were already done or in process. When that happened, he would smile and say, "Rey, this is becoming dangerous. It seems as if you can read my thoughts."

Rey loved to work with him and was sad to see him leave. A new manager arrived. In Rey's opinion, he could not fit in Eli's shoes. He was a completely different type of person. He didn't do much, and the little he did, he did himself. Rey had little to do, and her job became a nightmare. She cursed silently because there was nowhere to go.

After a few months, she decided to leave her job at the oil field. She didn't want to spoil the wonderful memories of her time in that magic place and leave with a bitter taste. She loved her job, and having Eli as her boss had had a lot to do with it. With all of the sadness, she knew that if she had no interest or satisfaction in her work, she would not last there. She also understood that her relationship with Avi had no future, and she needed to move on with her life. Avi would always have a warm spot in her heart for the wonderful year they'd had together and for what she'd received and learned from him. Shortly after she left the Suez oil field, she found a job with an American drilling company doing offshore seismic research on the Sinai Peninsula. The salary was great, was paid in US dollars, and came with a car and comfortable working hours. She was advised that the company could leave on a moment's notice, and if that happened, she would be paid for an extra month. She ended up working two and half months and was paid for four. They were headed for Mombasa, Kenya, with their drilling vessel, and they offered her a free ride if she was interested. Rey was thrilled by the invitation and the opportunity, but seeing the size of the boat, which was the size of a nutshell, chilled her enthusiasm, and she decided to pass and go on a journey of her own.

CHAPTER

Rey flew to South Africa and met an Israeli guy who offered her a job. She stayed for a year. It was quite an experience. She lived and worked in Johannesburg but traveled quite a bit. She looked at apartheid as something impossible to comprehend. Once, she went to a post office, and while she was standing in line, she noticed people looking at her. She did not understand why until someone whispered to her, "This post office is for non-Europeans only," which meant it was only for blacks. She found that expression ridiculous. She was also a non-European, wasn't she? Israel was not in Europe.

She once dated a guy and told him she was non-European, and he nearly fainted. Rey laughed and said, "I am from Israel, and if you look at a geographic map, you will see that Israel is between Asia and Africa."

"Yeah. Right," said the guy after recovering from the shock. "But it's not the same."

Yes, she thought, *it's not the same. Why do people hide behind masks instead of calling things what they really are?* Rey was young and naive, and obviously, the issue was far more complex than she realized.

South Africa's social life was like England's in the beginning of the nineteenth century. The formality and inflexibility were hard on her. She missed the freedom and openness she experienced in Israel. There were quite a few Israelis there, but she did not connect with them, and she did not meet anyone she really liked. She kept writing long letters to Avi, filled with longing, and he wrote to her too but not as often as she wanted. They both knew it was an impossible love.

Rey felt trapped. She had a wild affair with an Israeli airline pilot that lasted for a few months. They met whenever he arrived in Johannesburg. He wrote her letters that were as passionate as their meetings: "I am on my way to New York, flying at an altitude of thirty-five thousand feet. I wish you were here. I miss you terribly. I dream about you and desire you so much it drives me crazy. I will be arriving in Johannesburg next week, and we will paint the town red."

After saying all of that, he said to her one day, "Rey, I am married and have three kids. I can't afford to fall in love with you like this, and that is what is happening to me."

After a year, Rey decided to go back home. Upon her return, she found out that Marina, her friend from the oil field in Sinai, had left her job there too. She was now living in Tel Aviv and was looking for a roommate. It was perfect timing, and Rey moved in with her. Rey found a job, got used to living in Israel again, and started dating.

She was told about a late-night radio dating program named *Night Birds*. People could write to them, and based on the letters, they invited people to interviews. They then invited some of the individuals live on the air at the radio station to tell about themselves and what they were looking for in a mate. Rey applied and was accepted. Guys were calling the studio, and some of them got to be on the air. It was quite an experience. Finally, she chose one, Benny, and they went out for dinner, a treat of the radio station. Nothing came out of it, but all of the men who had not gotten to be on the air could write letters addressed to the radio station to be delivered to Rey. One of them was Haime, a GI stationed in his military service in Sinai. He listened to the program and was impressed with Rey. He was ten years younger and asked her to please give him a chance. He also mentioned that he was blond, blue-eyed, six feet tall, and very mature for his age.

Rey was determined not to date younger men. If she'd been asked why, she was not sure she could have explained. They continued corresponding, and Haime's letters became more and more detailed and intimate. In one of his letters, he wrote,

> I am an officer due to be discharged in a few weeks into a big question mark. During stormy period like ours, I, like every Israeli young man, go through the via dolorosa of desperate love of this beautiful, cruel country of ours, where some of my best friends were killed in battle—a country led by people who quite often make me want to puke. My problems are not different from those of other young men my age. And I am in a constant struggle between my will to contribute to this country and work on my own personal career between surrendering to patterns and the will to break all of the silly rules, between devoting myself to difficult tasks and saying, "Who gives a shit?" In short, being Israeli and young is difficult. And you come

into my life at this very moment, when I am disgusted with everything and have just ended another affair with a girl my age. I don't do too well with girls my age. And suddenly, there was this voice on the radio that stunned me. Every sentence was so full of life, original, and mature. This person was sensitive to her surroundings but did not surrender to them. I found myself talking out loud, saying, "Damn, where are girls like this? This is exactly what I am looking for, a woman with the courage to express things considered taboo." In short, you charmed me, girl. I don't know where in life I catch you right now—emotionally, that is—or what I, with our age difference, can offer you in the normal sense, but please give me a chance to know you.

Rey agreed, and they met. He was a good-looking young man. She told him up front that she was looking for someone to share her life with, and he was twenty-two years old, just at the beginning of his life's journey. They sat and talked for a few hours, and when they parted, she said she would think about it.

Haime continued to write her letters. He seemed to have the need to share with Rey what he was going through. He said he was amazed, while writing, at how he was opening up to her and revealing the emotional storm he was in.

He wrote one day,

It's too obvious that this time-to-think thing is your way of kind of being polite to avoid hurting my feelings. I can simply tell you that it has been a long time since I wanted something so badly and with such intensity, and I would give a lot to hear you say, "Haime, to hell with everything and everybody. Come to me." I am almost sorry that I do not have a few more years to bridge that damn age gap between us. I wish I was forty. What is happening to me? I feel like a silly teenager schoolboy in his first love affair. So que será, será. It's in your hands now.

This emotional storm continued as he kept writing.

Rey, it's a pleasure to be with a mature, wise woman with no age complexes—and good looking too. It's like they showed me how the woman I really want looks in real life, and it's clear to me that it will be almost impossible to take her back to her imaginary, abstract state now that I have met you. I really want you to be honest and tell me how you feel now. If you write to the address on this envelope, the letter will reach me wherever I am at all times. And finally, two things:

A. Try not to change in the next few years.

B. I could have loved you.

Amicably, Haime

PS Enclosed is a result of a moment inspiration, and I don't care if you think it's silly; you are the reason for this.

He had written a poem in which he described his feelings for her. The last part read,

You left me exposed to the wind,
without a place to hide,
and then you slammed the door
and left me in the dark.

Rey was stunned by the emotional state Haime was experiencing and his courage to stand there in front of her, exposed and vulnerable, and come out and say it all in writing without having a clue what would happen after the letter reached its destination, how she would react, and how she would feel about this whole thing. It seemed to her that despite all of the compliments, a relationship with him could be only a passionate summer love affair. Rey really wanted a long-term, serious relationship. She was tired of occasional excitements; she wanted someone by her side all along the way. She wanted to finally come home.

CHAPTER

JUST LIKE IN THE movies, a few months later, Rey and Mike met again ten years after they'd broken up. Both were single, and the timing was perfect.

This happened when Rey was sure she would never find a mate after her heart. She was tired of dating and tired of searching for the One. None of the men she dated seemed to be suitable for her, and at that point, she decided something was screwed up with her; she needed help. She decided to seek counseling.

Her therapist told her she was doing everything to avoid the screwed-up model of marriage her parents had provided. That was why she picked unsuitable men, and if she found one she really liked, he was married. It was a kind of survival.

Six months after she started her therapy, she and Mike met again. Tobi, a mutual friend with whom she'd kept in touch over the years, called her and asked if she wanted to go to the movies. "Sure," she said. "I'd love that."

"Okay," said Tobi. "I am bringing a friend."

"Should I bring one too?" she asked.

He said, "No, it's Mike."

"Oh, okay, great," she said, surprised. She had not seen Mike in a long time. Tobi had kept her posted every once in a while about Mike, and last she'd talked to him, he'd told her Mike was seeing a French girl, and it seemed to be serious.

"So what happened with the French girl?" Rey asked, and she immediately regretted the question.

"Well, I think it's over," he replied.

"Okay," she said. "See you tonight."

They went to a Woody Allen movie called *Love and Death*. Three months later, Rey and Mike moved in together. Mike, the love her life, the last person in the world she'd thought she would end up with, had appeared in her life again.

Finally, they got married. Rey decided she had to use all of the creative talents and tools she had to make this relationship work and to be aware of her bad habit of destroying everything. She loved Mike with all of her heart and soul and had no doubt about his love for her, but still, every time they had a fight, she was sure that was it. She believed he would tell her to pack her things and leave. This fear had been imprinted since her childhood. She wanted so much to be a good girl, but something always happened.

When her parents had divorced, they'd sent her to a boarding school for two years. When her mother had remarried, she and Rey's stepfather had brought her home, but things hadn't worked out, and they'd sent her to live with her uncle. A year later, when her aunt was pregnant and the baby was due, they'd told her she could not stay there any longer since there was not enough room. She figured she must have done something wrong, but she didn't know what. That was how this imprint was created. When Rey did something wrong, people sent her away.

But it didn't happen this time. She was there to stay. It was as if she'd broken the vicious circle. If something was wrong, she did whatever it took to make it right.

It took a few years, but eventually, she felt she had come home, this time to stay.

Fifteen years after they got married, Mike went to work one morning and never returned.

CHAPTER

Seven

Rey was on the way to her weekly workshop session. She'd come early because she wanted to have a few words with her teacher before everyone else arrived.

Upon her arrival at the studio, she found Batya preparing the place. Batya lit some candles and incense sticks that released the relaxing perfumed smoke special to that place. There, Rey had first experienced incense. It reminded her of a sanctuary, a place of worship. The two women hugged each other, and Batya said, "What's up?"

Rey looked at her for a long moment and said, "I want to have a relationship. When will I find a mate?"

Batya thought for a moment and said, "You will find a relationship when you will allow yourself to have one."

Batya gave self-awareness workshops, and her philosophy was "We create our own reality. If we say we want something and do not manage to realize our wishes, it is because we are not ready, or the current situation serves a purpose." Theoretically, Rey had checked this issue inside out.

When Mike was killed, Rey was forty-nine. They had gone to the United States, and they planned to stay for a year. That was the initial idea. Mike worked as a pilot for a small general aviation company, and Rey worked at a travel agency.

On the second day of Rosh Hashanah, at seven o'clock in the morning, the phone rang and woke up Rey. Carolyn was on the line. She was the operations manager of the company Mike worked for. "Rey," she said, "Mike left on a cargo flight to Flagstaff and did not arrive there."

Rey was still half asleep. She turned her head and saw Mike's side of the bed empty. "Mike left already," she said. "He should be there any minute now."

"No," Carolyn said, "you don't understand. Mike did not reach his destination. He never landed there as planned, and they lost contact with him."

The next thing Rey remembered was being at the Phoenix airport with her friends Stephanie and Joe. She didn't understand what they were doing there and did not remember how she'd gotten to the airport. They eventually took her to their home, and the authorities were informed of the airplane's disappearance. Rey didn't sleep that night. She prayed in every language to whomever was listening to her. *Maybe he is wounded, lying there, and can't move. Maybe he is unconscious. Maybe he is threatened by wild animals. Oh God, please watch over him. Don't let him suffer.*

She dozed off for a moment and woke up in a panic, covered with cold sweat, and she heard his voice calling for her. She lay there with open eyes, staring into the darkness. Her body was senseless. She didn't cry. *Please, God,* she said silently. *Please help me. Show me the way to deal with this. Now that I've found him again, you can't take him away from me. This is not fair.*

She fell asleep again until Stephanie woke her up. It was eleven o'clock in the morning, and two people waited for her in the living room, a man and a woman. It was exactly as she'd seen in the movies.

"Ma'am," the man said, "I'm afraid we have bad news. We found the airplane. Your husband is dead. He was killed on impact."

"Are you sure?" Rey asked.

The man and woman looked at each other, and after a moment, he replied, "Yes, ma'am, we are sure."

Everything that happened afterward, including the funeral, the weeklong shivah mourning ritual, and the children's arrival from Israel, was a vague memory. She could not believe Mike was gone. He'd left her forever. He could not do such a thing—abandon her alone in a foreign country. She felt a kind of déjà vu. That was what her parents had done to her. She'd believed she could trust him. But how could one be angry with the dead? They couldn't justify their actions or defend themselves; they were dead.

It was a month before her fiftieth birthday.

CHAPTER

Eight

FIFTEEN YEARS PASSED, AND thoughts of men and dating disappeared from her life. Rey the woman went into a deep emotional coma. She had no wish to change that and had no awareness of the issue. People tried to talk her into dating again and introduced her to some potential dates to no avail. Once, she took initiative when she saw a guy she thought was nice, but he happened to be gay. *My sensors are completely rusty,* she thought. *It's time for me to come back to live a full life with love, passion, and romance.*

Men did not court her, or if there were any, she hadn't noticed.

Batya thought for a moment and said, "I suggest you try circular breathing therapy. I know you are not too fond of this method and that it gives you the creeps, but maybe this major resistance is a good reason to try it. You must bypass blocks, resistance, and anxieties."

Rey knew a little about that therapy, and soon after Batya finished her studies, she gave her students a chance to get a taste of it. Rey had doubts about being able to do it consistently, but hey, what did she have to lose? The worst that could happen was that it wouldn't work out.

A few weeks after she started the therapy, she was on her way to work, and a man passed near her and said, "Good morning, pretty lady." He continued on.

Rey was surprised. She stopped for a moment and whispered, "Thank you."

Later that day, her phone rang. It was Sasha. He was in charge of one of the apartments in her building and took care of it while the owner was away. He wanted to come pay for the periodic maintenance fees, and he said he would drop by in the evening. Sasha was about fifty, well groomed, and not bad looking.

He came over and pulled a pack of bills from his pocket. He liked to pay cash. Rey went to the other room to get the receipt book and then sat at the table to fill in the details. Sasha approached her, knelt down, put his arms on her lap, looked right into her eyes, and said, "From the first day I saw you, I haven't stopped thinking about you. You are so pretty, so feminine."

Rey was in a state of shock. When she managed to catch her breath, she said, "Sasha, this is my house, and I want you to get up and leave now."

Sasha got up, took the receipt, and left without a word. Half an hour later, he called and said, "Rey, please don't hang up; just listen for a minute. I don't know what happened to me. I didn't mean to offend you or hurt your feelings. I said exactly what I feel. I am asking you to please have coffee with me so I can apologize properly."

"I am not saying anything," she said.

"Then please just call back, even if it's to say no. Please."

She said okay and hung up.

She called Batya, all shaken up, and told her what had happened.

"What was that all about?" Rey said. "This guy is completely nuts and out of his mind. Don't you think?"

"My darling," replied Batya, "welcome back to the world of the living."

CHAPTER

MOST OF THE GIRLS who worked with Rey in the office were in their thirties. They considered her a friend and invited her to join them on an occasional night out. They shared their dating experiences and stories about the guys they met. Mali told them about a gorgeous guy she'd met recently. They had gone out once, and she really hoped he would call her again.

"Where did you meet?" Rey asked.

"On the internet, on a dating website."

Rey's computer skills were almost nonexistent, and she knew even less about the current dating game. "How do you do it?" she asked.

"Well," said Mali, "you have to Google *dating*, surf a bit, check the various dating sites to see which one you like, and then register and create a profile."

Rey had no clue what she was talking about. It must have shown, because Mali said, "When you decide, let me know, and I will show you how this works."

Mali kept her promise and sat with Rey to show her the ropes. They chose a dating website, registered, and started filling in the details, answering the various questions. With every detail Rey added, she felt as if she were taking off another piece of clothing—kind of a virtual striptease.

When they had to fill in Rey's date of birth, Mali said, "You look much younger than your age. You could easily take ten years off. Basically, it is important to fill in valid information. Eventually, you will meet some of the guys. But you can play around with your age. It's also important to write what you are looking for, despite the fact that some of the visitors do not bother to read the details or disregard certain info when it suits them."

They finished creating the profile, and Rey felt uncomfortable. She was not sure online dating was something she wanted to do.

"Okay," Mali said, "now you only have to add photographs and wait twenty-four hours until they approve the pictures and the text."

"Photographs? What photographs?" Rey asked.

"Yours. Photos of you. Without photographs to back up your profile, there is a good chance nobody will visit your profile. Men want to see the lady behind the information. Wouldn't you?"

Rey felt as if she were about to go through the worst humiliation of her life. First, she had to admit in front of the whole world that she couldn't find a mate, and on top of that, she needed to put a face to her profile. *It's like I am on display in a window in the mall,* she thought. *Men are walking by, checking me out and passing judgment. It really is the end of the world.*

Rey was not much into taking photos and did not have any suitable recent pictures. Further, she did not know how to put them up on her profile. She had to get used to the idea that every Tom, Dick, and Harry who hung around that website could freely read her profile, examine her, and write who knew what. It was scary.

"Okay, no pictures for now," she said. "We'll see what happens later."

Rey had to learn how to get into her account and find her way around inside. She made notes of the technical details regarding entering her profile, reading messages, replying, and checking for visitors.

A couple of days later, she decided to log in to check if there was any activity. After a few attempts, she managed to get in and saw that there were no messages. There was one visitor, and he didn't have a photograph either. She checked his profile and found it unappealing.

It took her a few months to get the hang of the website, and finally, she gathered the courage to ask a friend to take some pictures of her and put them in her profile.

"That's it," Rey said. "I am out of the closet and lived to tell about it." Her friend wished her good luck.

Rey continued with her breathing therapy, and the change occurred as if unintentionally. Her clothing style became younger. She wore mostly jeans and T-shirts, which were her favorite and showed her long legs. One of her friends said, "Hey, Rey, now we can see that you have a body."

Things started happening. She found herself on the dating website more often to check the activity, visitors, and messages, and she felt a sense of anticipation.

One day she got a message from a guy named Yossi. She went into his profile and saw that he was twenty-eight years old. *What does he want?* she thought. *Can't you see the age difference? Perhaps he is a gigolo looking for a sugar mommy. Probably wants to be a kept man.* She erased his message immediately.

Rey started thinking maybe the whole thing was a mistake—to post her picture and advertise personal information. What if she met someone she knew? What would she do? What a humiliation that would be. Then a voice inside said, *Hey, babe, what would that someone be doing on the dating site anyway? He would be looking for someone too, right?*

Yeah, she thought, *but it's not the same.*

Come on, Rey. Stop it. You are here now, and everyone can see you. You're a tall, good-looking woman—quite a catch. And that's it.

Rey woke up on a day off: Election Day 2006. She planned to go vote to fulfill her civic duty, and then she could do anything she pleased. Perhaps she would go to the beach or maybe to the open market.

She made herself a cup of coffee and went out to sit on the veranda. A few moments later, she decided to check the computer to see if there was any action there. It had become a ritual to go see what was cooking in the "sandbox," as she referred to it. There was one message, and Rey went in to check the profile. Izzy was thirty-four years old, separated, and six feet tall, and he lived in Rishon. There was a picture too. He was a nice-looking guy wearing glasses. *What is it,* she thought *with these young men? What is it they want with me?*

He'd written, "I have nothing clever to say except that I want to meet you."

She saw that he was online and thanked him for the compliment.

He replied instantly, "Please send your phone number, and I will call."

Rey found herself sending her phone number without hesitation. He called a few moments later. Rey felt her heart beating fast.

"Good morning," he said. "It's Izzy."

"Good morning," she replied.

"Thanks for sending your phone number. How are you this morning?"

"Fine, thank you," she replied, feeling a bit short of breath. "And you?"

"I am fine."

"Did you vote already?" she asked.

"Not yet. I am working today. I shall go in the afternoon."

"Why did you approach me?" she asked.

"I like you, and I want to get to know you," he said.

"Are you aware of the age difference between us?"

"Of course," he said.

"So what makes a thirty-four-year-old man approach a woman my age?" *Except for the obvious reasons*, she wanted to add, but she didn't.

"Look, I know what you are thinking, and I will not lie. You are an attractive and beautiful woman, and I have a feeling that it will be interesting talking to you. I can tell you I've never had a relationship based on sex only with a woman. I think that after once or twice, you lose interest."

"You wrote that you are separated. What does that mean exactly?"

"My wife and I want to get a divorce, but because our kids are small and quite attached to me, we decided to make it gradually, one step at a time. So in the meantime, I live at home in a separate bedroom, and I come and go as I please."

Yeah, she thought. *Separate bedrooms with a connecting door.*

"I come and go as I please but continue with my share of caring for the children and spend quality time with them, hoping I will be able to explain to them what is going to happen."

Sounds interesting, Rey thought.

The conversation kept on for another hour or so, and then Izzy said, "I have to go now; I have a meeting. I will call you later if that's okay with you."

Rey remained seated, trying to figure out what had just happened in the last hour and a half. A man thirty years younger wanted to meet her, and he sounded normal and even smart and sensitive. He did not look bad at all. She was playing along with all of this. What was wrong with her? Had she gone completely out of her mind? Where was her common sense? It seemed she had lost it completely.

She went to take a shower to wash away the confusion and the anxiety. She stood for a long time under the water; she couldn't even think straight. She felt overwhelmed. This situation was something completely new and strange.

She got dressed and decided to go vote and then go to the beach near the dolphinarium. She loved to sit on the beach to watch the infinite blue and smell the salty air, which she found intoxicating and which gave her peace and tranquility.

After she'd voted, when she got to the beach, she was still caught up in her new experience, unaware of her surroundings. She sat on one of the stone benches on the promenade and tried to figure out what was happening in her life.

Her ringing cell phone interrupted her thoughts. It was Izzy.

"Hi, Rey. Sorry I had to cut off our conversation. Like I said, I had a business meeting in the office. It looks as if the rest of the day will be quiet. There is no one else here. I have a lot of paperwork, and I get quite productive when it's quiet here. Where are you? I hear background noises."

"I am at the promenade near the beach. I went to vote and then came here."

Izzy told her about himself and asked Rey an occasional question. They talked until late afternoon. Finally, he said, "I want to meet you, but it will be possible only in a few days. My wife is away on a business trip, and I am with the kids."

Very good, Rey thought. *Everything is so intense that I can hardly think.* She decided not to share this new event with anyone, afraid of what she felt and that the magic might evaporate.

Over the next few days, they spent a lot of time on the phone. They had long conversations into the night, and Rey felt excited. With the excitement came anxiety. What if he didn't like her? During one of their conversations, she asked him about it, and he replied instantly, "That won't happen. Someone who has such a voice and whom I can talk with about all these things—there's no way I will not like her."

Rey felt her level of anxiety rising. *Now I'll have to live up to these expectations.* When was the last time she'd been with a man? When was the last time she'd undressed in front of a man? The last time had been with Mike, and that had been many years ago. She could not think about their meeting in a romantic way because if she did, she would chicken out and run away before it started. *Oh God,* she thought, *I don't remember ever thinking about things like that. How do I look? How does my body look? I am not twenty anymore—too fat and maybe too old. I'll have to buy new lingerie. Which clothes? What is it going to be like?*

What was the worst that could happen? She would ask to undress in the dark. But what if it happened during the day or if he asked to see her naked? What if she did not turn him on because she was an elderly woman? *Rey, darling,* she finally said to herself, *if he is looking for a woman with a sixteen-year-old's body, he has to look for a sixteen-year-old girl. You have to get out of this horror movie. It's not the end of the world, and Izzy is not your future groom who will run away and leave you alone at the altar in front of all of the guests, right? So cut it out.*

She decided to call Batya, who suggested they meet. Rey arrived at the studio and told Batya about Izzy and all that had happened in the last few days. Batya looked at her for a moment and then said, "Okay, so it's happening to you. It's important for you to remember that until now, no man has made a pass at you, or at least you have not noticed, and there was this thing with Sasha and now Izzy. Darling, you finally woke up. We did a jump start on a system that was completely out of commission. You are going back to being a woman again; you radiate your femininity, and men are reacting. It's good, actually. It's very good. I suggest you go slowly, and more importantly, pay attention to how you feel. At this point, do only what feels right to you, not what you think someone expects you to do. If you feel something is happening too fast or too soon, stop. It's essential to keep things at the rate and balance that are right and suitable for you at this time."

A week after they'd first spoken, Izzy and Rey decided to meet at Rey's place. He arrived late in the afternoon. She took a peek from the terrace; she wanted to catch a glimpse before he came up. She managed to see that his hair was short, almost shaved, and he wore glasses. He rang the intercom, and she told him to come to the fifth floor. She debated whether she should open the door or wait until he rang the doorbell.

He rang before she made a decision. Rey opened the door. She was excited. She was afraid her heart would jump out of her body. Izzy was a tall, big man. He walked in and gave Rey a big, long hug. Rey invited him to come in and have a seat. There was an awkward moment during which they were both silent. It was weird after all of the conversations they'd had.

"Did you find the address easily?" Rey asked.

"Yes," he said. "I know this part of town well."

Rey said she was going to bring out a bottle of wine if that was okay, and he nodded. She noticed him examining the apartment and her.

She placed the bottle on the table and asked him if he cared to open it. He said he'd leave it to the lady of the house. Rey pulled out the cork and poured red wine into two tall glasses. They clinked the glasses and drank. They resumed their conversation, and the awkwardness disappeared almost as it had on the phone. Izzy moved to sit next to Rey. He patted her cheeks and said, "Your cheeks are flushed. Are you hot?" He did not wait for her answer—he kissed her on the lips.

They kissed and went up to the bedroom on the second floor. Rey found herself undressing freely, as if she had done this in front of Izzy many times, and got under the blanket. Izzy took off his clothes but left his briefs on and got under the blanket too. They kissed again, and then Rey said, "We're doing safe sex, right?" She had a box of condoms in her chest drawer. A friend had given it to her with his blessing.

She saw the expression on his face, and he said, "I prefer without a condom. I want to feel you."

Rey freaked out. The truth was, she'd never had sex with condoms. At the time, she used birth control pills, and nobody knew of HIV.

Eventually, there was no need for a condom—Izzy couldn't get it up. Rey felt as if she were in a horror movie again. She did not turn him on—that was it. She wanted to get out of bed and jump out the window. When they got out of bed, Izzy said, as if joking, "Tomorrow you'll tell your girlfriends that you were in bed with a thirty-four-year-old man, and nothing happened."

What does he mean? she thought. *Now it's my fault?* This was not how she had imagined sex after all these years. *What a disappointment.*

As it turned out, Izzy was on medication for high blood pressure, and it sometimes affected his sexual performance. The truth was that his wand was a miniwand, but it didn't matter anymore. Izzy left, and Rey was left with herself. She still thought that what had happened was her fault.

They stayed in touch on the phone. Izzy was the one who usually called. They never mentioned that embarrassing incident again. One morning Rey called him, and when he answered, he said, "Rey, you can't call whenever you want."

She hung up without saying a word.

He called back after a few minutes and said, "I'm sorry. I am with the kids now, and I can't talk."

"You could have said, 'I'll call you back,' or something."

"Sorry," he replied. "I was all stressed out. I will come this evening, and we'll talk, if it's okay with you."

"I will let you know later," she said, and she hung up.

When he arrived that evening, Rey was still upset and hurt. "There is no way you can talk to me in that tone of voice," she said. "If you have a problem, tell me about it. Besides, you act like a married man, not a separated one. This whole situation does not seem right to me at all."

"You are right," he said. "I am sorry. It will not happen again."

Rey forgave him. She didn't know why. What was there in this kind of relationship for her? He was not a potential mate. He was not rich, so he couldn't take her around the world. Sex didn't seem to be one of his strong suits, and he seemed to be on a short leash. What was she doing?

"Listen," he said suddenly. "I have some vacation days coming that I have to use now; otherwise, I will lose them. Why don't we go somewhere for a long weekend—say, Greece or Italy? What do you think?"

Rey looked at him, thinking, *Where did this come from?*

"Are you inviting me?" she asked.

"No," he replied. "I don't have the means to pay for both of us, but I thought we could each pay our way and have a fun weekend with no distractions."

"Thanks for the invitation," she replied. "I'll have to sleep on it."

They decided to take the trip together. Izzy was thrilled that she agreed to go. He said he would work on the itinerary, and then they would go over it together. Since Mike had died, she had not traveled with anyone. Mike had always planned everything, and during the long years after his death, Rey had traveled alone. She chose the destinations, planned everything, booked hotels, met interesting people, and had a great time. This was the first time she was willing to release control and let someone else do all of the planning.

Their flight to Florence left at midnight. They landed at dawn and took a taxi to the hotel. It was early morning. Check-in was usually around two o'clock. They went to the reception, and Rey gave their names. The receptionist, a young woman, looked at Rey and then at Izzy, and after a moment's hesitation, she asked in English, "How do you prefer your sleeping arrangements in the room?"

Rey replied quietly, "We prefer a room with one large, comfortable bed, please."

The receptionist lowered her eyes. "Yes, ma'am, of course."

Rey added, "We were on a night flight and would appreciate it if we can get a room ASAP."

"Yes," the girl answered, "I'll see what I can do."

They got their room after an hour, left their things there, and came downstairs to the cafeteria for a strong espresso. They called the car rental company and asked for their car to be delivered to the hotel. They ate a rich breakfast and were on their way according to Izzy's plan. They visited the city; the famous opera house; the Duomo, the central cathedral, one of the most beautiful in Italy; and the colorful Nabili quarter's cafés and galleries.

In the early afternoon, Rey suggested they return to the hotel for a break to rest and be ready for the evening. When they entered the room, Rey was nervous. They had not made love since that first time, and she wondered if she wanted to because she was attracted to him or because she needed to be sure that she was okay and that there was nothing else involved.

She went to take a shower, and when she came out, she found Izzy asleep on the bed. She slipped under the covers and fell asleep too.

When she woke, it was already after seven o'clock in the evening. She heard that Izzy was in the shower and wondered if she should bring up the issue. *What if it changes the whole atmosphere and spoils everything? On the other hand, you can't let fear manage your life.* She knew for sure she needed to bring up the subject—but not now. She would let it be for now. *We'll see what happens tonight.*

They went to see one of Da Vinci's most famous works of art: *The Last Supper.* The painting showed Jesus during the Passover dinner, when he predicted to his apostles that one of them would betray him and turn him over to the Romans. A series of reconstructions had damaged the painting, but recent work had been done to overcome the damage, and today the painting was spectacular. The recent movie *The Da Vinci Code* had helped restore the painting's ancient glory. The painting was on display at the Dominican monastery situated near Santa Maria delle Grazie.

They had cappuccino and tried the famous Italian gelato.

"The truth is," Izzy said, "the ice creams in Israel are as good."

"Yes," Rey replied, "especially the Italian ones."

In the evening, they went to a seafood and pasta restaurant the hotel recommended. The place was pleasant. There were small tables with white tablecloths, which created a comfortable atmosphere, as if the guests were seated at a family affair in a backyard.

The food was excellent. Rey ordered langoustines in their shells, and Izzy ordered pasta with shrimp. Rey enjoyed her langoustines, which were cooked to perfection, despite the simple receipt. The secret was always in the quality of the product. She cracked them with her hands, and at one point, she noticed Izzy was staring at her. She could not figure out the reason.

The wine the waiter recommended was excellent. They ordered one tiramisu to share and walked back to the hotel.

"Rey," Izzy said suddenly, "I want to say something, and please don't be offended."

"Okay," she said, feeling the tension rising in her body. *He will probably make an excuse and ask me not to make any sexual advances, and what then?*

"When we were seated at the restaurant," he said, "I saw you eating the seafood with your hands, and I felt uncomfortable because it seems like a respectable restaurant, and I thought it was not appropriate."

Rey was relieved that his concern was not about *that* issue. She replied, "First, thank you for sharing your thoughts and feelings with me. And as for your comment, seafood in their shells are eaten with your hands since there is no way you can eat them with a fork and a knife. In addition, if you noticed, on the table were little bowls with water and a slice of lemon in them."

"Yes," he replied.

"Well, those are specifically for dipping your fingers after you're done eating."

"Okay," Izzy said, smiling, embarrassed a little. "I have learned something new today."

They walked into the hotel, and the reception clerk greeted them with a big smile and asked, "So how was the restaurant?"

"Magnificent," Rey replied.

The clerk gave a thumbs-up and said, *"Buona notte"* (Good night).

They went up to their room, and Rey went into the bathroom to brush her teeth. She came out wearing a T-shirt and got into bed. Izzy was sitting by the desk, checking the itinerary for tomorrow's trip to Verona. They were planning to leave right after breakfast. They'd head for Verona to visit the house of Romeo, Juliet's lover.

Izzy undressed and got into bed. There was tension in the air, or at least that was how Rey felt. She decided to bring up the subject. "I feel uncomfortable," she said. "There is something between us that prevents closeness. I don't know where the problem is, and I don't know how to handle it."

He came close to her and kissed her on the cheek. "Look, I told you that I have high blood pressure, and lately, I've started taking medication. One of the side effects is sexual malfunction. The doctor said it might take from a few weeks to a few months. Despite the fact that you know about it, until this is over, I don't wish to go through that unfortunate experience again; it's quite embarrassing. I hope you understand and forgive me."

Yeah right, Rey thought to herself. *It would have been nice if you'd told me about your little problem before our trip.* She kept that thought to herself and said, "Okay, just remind me when we reach Verona to put my hand on Juliet's statue's left breast and ask for her blessing, according to the custom."

During the coming days, Rey managed to put the sex issue aside and enjoy the trip. The weather was beautiful. They reached Venice, where Rey bought two of the beautiful masks from the famous carnival. She'd never visited that part of Italy. The planning of the trip was perfect, and Izzy was an excellent driver with a built-in sense of navigation. It was time to go back home.

They took a cab to the airport for the flight back and went to the Alitalia counter. The flight was delayed. After a few hours, they boarded the airplane and took their seats. At some point, Rey noticed one of the flight attendants paying quite a bit of attention to Izzy. She was young and pretty, and Izzy was enjoying the fuss. Rey thought, *Great, girl. Go for it. Invite him to your hotel room so you can enjoy his sexual performance.* Then she said to herself, *Oh, Rey, don't be a bitch.*

CHAPTER

AFTER THEIR RETURN, IZZY was busy with his job and the kids, and the relationship seemed to dissolve. Rey lost interest. His life was too complicated for her. It had been a fling, an experience on the learning path. She spent quite some time online, and she learned more about how things worked on websites in general and the dating site in particular. She felt like a child who'd just learned to read and couldn't read enough books. She was eager to learn more, and the fact that she'd overcome the technological barrier gave her much pleasure and pride. She felt confident and knew she could do anything she put her mind to.

Flirting online became quite a thrill; she enjoyed the attention and the new game she'd discovered. Visiting the sites became a morning ritual, along with her coffee. She was eager to see who'd visited her profile and if anyone had left a message, and she found herself spending time chatting online. She learned the website's slang, including the actual meaning of *cybersex*. She was not bothered anymore by young men approaching her; she enjoyed the flirting and the attention.

One of those men was a thirty-six-year-old guy from Haifa called Yaron. He did not have a photograph in his profile, but he said he liked her a lot and asked if she would send him her email address. Rey sent him her email. First, he wrote about himself. He was working for a CPA firm and was just about to take his final CPA exams. Rey wrote a bit about herself. She liked him because he had a way with words. He was articulate, had a rich vocabulary, and used descriptive phrases. There was a sexual energy hidden in his words. Rey sensed it, and it scared her. She had never experienced this kind of relationship: a man she did not know was courting her with growing intensity, and she didn't even know what he looked like.

He wrote about how much he longed to meet her, and she felt an unfamiliar excitement. He sent twenty or thirty emails with graphic descriptions of how he felt about her, how she made him feel, and what their first meeting would be like. One message said,

> You know, I can't concentrate at work. I think about you constantly, trying to imagine you, and I have palpitations. I am in constant excitement. I had a dream that our first meeting was at the airport. I bought us two tickets to Rio de Janeiro to go to the Carnival. I sent them to you with a messenger and enclosed a note that we would meet on the plane. That is where our date started. Upon our arrival in Rio, we took a cab to the hotel. We couldn't wait; we made love in the cab. It was hot and humid, with no air-conditioning in the cab, but we didn't pay any attention. I feel things I've never felt before. You excite my imagination. I'm going out of my mind.

Rey read the email a number of times and felt that her body was coming alive. She didn't know if she should be stimulated or ashamed. For her, it was a primal experience—exciting and scary at the same time. There was a gap between love like in the movies, with slow courting and patience, and this was enormous. *Is this a cheap thrill?* she asked herself. The answer came: *No, my dear, it's the desert coming alive. It's as simple as that.*

Interestingly, during that whole week of intense, erotic correspondence, neither asked for the other's phone number. It seemed both felt comfortable in their anonymity.

A few days later, Rey found a short email in her box from Yaron: "I'm dying to see you. Say when."

She waited with the reply. She was not sure what she wanted. She finally replied, "I want to hear your voice first. Here is my number. Call me."

He wrote back, "Okay. I'm going to a business meeting with a client. I'll call you in about an hour."

She replied with a smiley face.

After an hour, her phone rang. "Hello?" she said.

"Hi, Rey. It's Yaron."

"Hi," she replied. "How are you?"

"I don't know," he said, "I am very excited, and I can't wait to see you."

His voice was high-pitched, not what she had expected. He said he was in the office and had to be brief but would call later. "Would tomorrow evening be a good time for us to meet?" he asked.

"Where?" she asked.

"I'll take the train," he said. "Choose a place, and I'll be there."

They decided to meet at a café on Rothschild Boulevard at seven thirty.

"I'll call you later." He said bye and hung up.

Rey remained in her seat without a motion. Things were going too fast. She felt overwhelmed with thoughts and feelings. This was strange to her—something totally different. Everything she thought she'd known about relationships between men and women was in the past—gone, nonexistent. What she used to know seemed like a million years ago. She felt that was sad on one hand and exciting on the other. She could not ignore the feeling of excitement and anticipation she felt at going into the unknown.

Yaron called again after a few hours. Rey noticed the gap between the rich language he used in his emails and the language he used on the phone. The thought was there for a moment and then disappeared.

The next day, Rey left the house at seven o'clock in the evening. She decided a good walk would balance her energies with the excitement she felt at going to meet Yaron.

She arrived a few minutes early, walked into the café, scanned it, and chose a table with a good view of the entrance. A waitress approached and gave her a menu. Rey thanked her and said she was waiting for someone. She looked at the menu for a moment, and when she looked up, she saw a young man standing by her table. "Yaron?" she asked.

He smiled and took a seat. He looked about twenty-two years old—like a boy. He was not tall and was altogether quite disappointing. *Okay*, she thought, *now I have to find a way to make the time as pleasant as possible.* She asked if he'd had trouble finding the place, and he said he had arrived in the city a few hours ago because he'd wanted to do some shopping. He liked brand names and came every so often to Tel Aviv to buy stuff.

Rey listened to him talk about Armani, Gucci, Lacoste, shoes, watches, and perfumes. She thought he talked like a teenager trying to impress the girls. More than that, she wondered, *Where is the rich language he used in his emails?* Was it possible the one she'd met was not the same one who'd written the emails? Had someone else written them for him? Or maybe he'd copied them from somewhere. The thought reminded her of the story of Cyrano de Bergerac, the French officer who wrote love letters for one of his soldiers who was illiterate and could not write. When the soldier finally met his love, she could not understand where the charming man who'd written all of the passionate, wonderful love letters had disappeared to.

They sat in the café for about an hour. Yaron said he really liked her and would like to plan a date with more time and more privacy.

Rey said she had to go, and they would talk about it later. They walked out of the café. Yaron kissed her on the cheek, and they said goodbye.

On the way home, Rey thought, *What a bummer. Total disappointment. Okay, sweetie,* she told herself, *what did you expect? When you mess with boys, that's what you get. Oh well. Don't be so hard on yourself; you are in uncharted territory on an exploratory journey. You win a few; you lose a few. That is the idea in experimenting with new things, isn't it?*

It was clear to her she had no interest in meeting Yaron again whatsoever. She would have to find a way to overcome that hurdle elegantly. One thing was important to her in her dating: no matter whom she met, she would always treat the man with respect and dignity. The fact that she didn't like him as a mate did not make him less respectable.

When Rey arrived home, she went right to her computer. There were new messages, new gentlemen callers, and new excitements. She was familiar now with dating-world lingo, the expressions men used, and which direction they were heading—a totally new language with hidden agendas. They would say, "Hello, pretty woman," "Good evening, princess," or "Hey, sexy lady." Rey felt like Alice in Wonderland. She'd landed in a reality she hadn't known existed—and it felt wonderful and exciting.

Screw all those who tell me that it's all fake and an illusion and that all the men really want is to get me into bed. Okay, Rey asked herself, *what do you want now? What are you looking for?* The answer came rather quickly: *To have a good time, experience new things I have never done before, and be a woman again.*

Later that evening, she received an email from Yaron, complimenting her on how pretty she looked. He wanted them to meet again for a longer date so they could be together. Rey decided to wait with the reply. She had to think about how to refuse politely. *Thanks, but no thanks.*

Rey did not have many friends. She was not one of those who had friends from way back in school and her military service. Most of the people in her life where those she'd met in the past ten years, and most of them were much younger. However, she had two girlfriends she'd met along the way who were closer to her age: Tammy and Yael. Bothe were divorced after years of marriage. They met every now and then and had a good time. Rey did not share her experiences with them; she felt her love life was her private territory. The only one who knew about Rey's adventures was Batya. Rey confided in her because she knew Batya would provide her with honest, unprejudiced opinions.

Rey started her own blog on a social website and wrote posts frequently. She had virtual friends there, and she started spending quite some time online. This was another new world she discovered, full of excitement and a sense of accomplishment for her in overcoming the technological barrier of the digital era. In writing, she discovered a way to express feelings locked inside of her she hadn't even known existed, especially after Mike's death. "The Woman Who Came Back from the Cold" was the name of a post she wrote in her blog. It was a description of her coming back to life as a woman. The amazing feedback she received surprised her.

> I was a woman in a frozen point in time.
> Chambers of my heart were gray,
> Sediments of burning lava gone cold,
> Turned into stone.
> One heart closed, locked,
> Locked in a mute soul.
> A beam of light penetrates through a crack in the stone.
> Its light, coming from the heart, chased the gray and cold.
> It touched the stone, which suddenly softened,
> Allowing the soul to soar again.
> It did take off into the horizon,
> Into the sunny blue skies and the soft clouds.
> The world was full of color,
> Of taste and the smell of spring,
> Something she'd forgotten from times long passed.
> It was a little scary,
> All so different now.

Confident in her body,
To quench her thirst at last,
She's free to choose direction.
No limits, none for her.
A steady hand extended
The rhythm slow or fast.
Abundance of temptations
To make up for the past.

The first time someone asked her to be friends on the website, the request reminded her of her feelings in third grade. But gradually, she learned the language used on the website, and now she had quite a few friends there. When Omer asked for them to be friends, she checked his profile. He was thirty-eight years old and a winemaker, was divorced, and lived in Hod Hasharon.

They spent some time on the chat feature, and he asked if he could get her phone number. Before she gave it to him, she asked if he was aware of the age difference between them.

"Of course," he said. "I went over your profile with much interest more than once."

"And why did you contact me?" she said.

"I would like to explain this on the phone, if it's okay with you."

Rey sent her phone number, and he called immediately.

"Look," he said, "I adore older women. They are smart, wise, and well balanced. They are good friends, they don't like hanging out in noisy bars, their biological clock is not an issue, and you can talk with them about almost any subject. They enjoy a nice evening in a restaurant and a good conversation over a glass of wine. That is my personal experience."

"I understand you are one of those who believes flattery will take you a long way," she said.

"No. Really, I am telling you the truth as I see it, and if something happens between us, you will find out for yourself."

They talked for a bit longer, and then Omer asked if she would like for them to meet. Rey said yes. He sounded like quite a guy, and they decided to meet the next evening. Omer said he would pick her up, and they would go out for dinner. "Any preferences?" he asked.

"Surprise me," Rey replied.

"Okay," he said. "A woman after my own heart."

Rey was excited as the evening date approached. She was debating what to wear. Should she wear jeans and a blouse or make a grand entrance with her little black dress and high heels? Finally, she decided. "Well," she said, "we'll see how I feel tomorrow."

Omer had a picture in his profile, but it was taken from a distance. He seemed tall and handsome. Omer called the next afternoon. She saw his number on the screen and thought, *He probably had a change of heart. He will make up something, suggest we meet another time, and disappear.* She answered and heard his voice.

"Hi. How are you?" he asked.

"Good," she said. "And you?"

"Wonderful. Just calling to see if we are still on for tonight and make sure there has been no change on your end."

"No," she replied. "No changes, but it's nice of you to ask."

"Thank you," he said. "I don't take anything for granted."

"Yes," Rey said, "I think so too." She gave him her address.

"I'll pick you up at seven thirty. I'll call from downstairs, if it's okay with you."

"Perfect," Rey replied.

"Okay, see you tomorrow. Bye." He hung up.

Rey was thrilled. *It seems,* she thought, *chivalry is still alive and kicking. We'll see where this leads us.*

When she returned from work, she opened her closet and stood there, debating again. She decided she would make the grand entrance another time. If something came out of the meeting, she would have another opportunity. She chose black jeans, a white silk shirt, and black moccasins. She went into the shower and stood there for a long time to relax her body from all of the excitement she felt. She did not know what to expect and decided just to savor the moment and enjoy the unfolding.

She got dressed, looked in the mirror, and said, "Rey, you don't look too bad at all. As a matter of fact, you look like a million dollars." She put on some makeup, including blush, and sprayed some of her favorite perfume, Narciso Rodriguez, onto her pulse spots. She decided to wear her gold-and-black feather earring. She liked to wear only one earring; she found it exotic. Her golden earrings were the only ones she wore as a pair.

It was 7:25 p.m., and her phone rang. *Punctual too,* she thought.

"I am right in front of the entrance," he said.

"Coming down," she replied. *It looks too good to be true,* she thought to herself while grabbing her purse and jean jacket and heading downstairs.

Omer was outside the entrance, just as he'd said. He got out of the car and said, "Good evening. I am Omer."

"And I am Rey," she replied.

He hugged her lightly and kissed her on the cheek. He wore a wonderful, masculine perfume with a light presence, just the way she liked it. Rey got into the car and buckled up with her heart pounding strongly.

"The picture in your profile does not do you justice," he said. "You are much more beautiful in real life."

"Thanks," she said. "If it was not dark in the car, you could see me blush."

"That means that your soul is still in its twenties."

Rey did not know how to handle all of this and said, "You have to give me a break with all of the compliments because if you go on, I will faint."

Omer laughed. "Okay, okay, whatever you say."

"Where are we going?" she asked.

"I hope you like seafood, but even if you don't, there are plenty of other things to choose from."

"I love seafood," she said.

"Great. I was pretty sure you would. There is a restaurant in Jaffa by the sea with good food that I find quite enjoyable."

They arrived at the restaurant and were seated. The place was nice and not too crowded. They got a table facing the sea and somewhat apart from the other tables. *Perfect choice*, she thought.

The waitress came over, and Omer asked her to give them a minute. They checked the menu. Rey ordered fried calamari, and Omer ordered seafood in butter and wine. "What kind of wine would you like?" he asked.

"Since you are the connoisseur, I trust your choice."

He ordered a bottle of fumé blanc.

"Fumé blanc is one of my favorite white wines," she said.

He smiled and said, "So far so good."

Rey nodded. "Yes, it is."

The food was good; the wine was perfect; and Omer, she discovered, was an interesting person. He told her he'd had an affair with a married woman that had lasted a year. He'd loved her very much but realized there was no future for them and decided to break up. He was still licking his wounds.

"A new love is a good way of healing a lost one indeed," he said, "but now the fear of getting hurt gets in the way."

"Tell me about it," she said.

He looked at her for a moment and said, "You have a story too?"

"Who doesn't?" she said. "But not tonight." She lifted her glass and said, "Cheers to this wonderful wine and to those who made it; to new people; to new, exciting experiences; and to the good life."

"Cheers," Omer said, and he finished the wine in his glass.

They finished eating and sat there for a little longer, and then Omer suggested they take a stroll along the boardwalk. She agreed willingly. The sea was calm, and there was a light breeze with the salty smell that Rey thought was one of the most intoxicating smells. "Nice," she said. "Very pleasant."

The sky was dotted with stars that looked like little diamonds on black velvet. Omer stopped for a moment, looked at Rey, stepped closer, and kissed her lightly on her lips. Rey closed her eyes, afraid to open them. She kept them closed so the magic would not vanish.

He kissed her again. This time, it was a long, passionate kiss. She didn't remember when'd she felt such excitement. His lips were soft. He kissed her with short kisses at first, and they turned gradually longer and deeper. Rey felt dizzy and experienced a sense of floating. Then he held her tightly and kissed her with a long, demanding kiss. They were both silent for a moment until Omer broke the silence.

He said, "It felt just as I imagined it. I have a wild imagination, and I tend to imagine things before they happen. I am very seldom wrong."

Rey didn't know what to say, but she did not have to say anything. Omer kissed her again. The guy was quite a kisser, and she felt at that moment as if she could kiss him forever.

They kept walking silently, each with his or her own thoughts, until they reached the car and got in. Omer drove toward Rey's house and stopped in front of the entrance. "Would you like to come up for a cup of coffee?" she said.

"You are asking so nicely—how can I refuse?"

They got into the elevator. Rey prayed she would not meet any of the neighbors. She was still busy thinking, *What is it that this young, good-looking man finds in me? Is this all because he wants to get me into bed? And what do you want, Rey? What could be wrong with a passionate night with someone like Omer? Yes, and how are you going to tell him that you have not been with a man for quite some time and probably have forgotten how to handle yourself in bed? Wait. Handle? In bed? Where is this coming from? You don't handle yourself in bed; you enjoy yourself. Just be yourself. Close your eyes, enjoy the moment, and let him lead the way.*

"Do you want coffee, or would you prefer something stronger?" she asked as they entered her apartment. "We can continue with white wine; there is an open bottle. Or maybe something stronger, like bourbon, if you wish."

"Yeah, bourbon is good. Like I said, you are a woman after my own heart. Beautiful and knows her drinks."

Rey brought out the bourbon and two glasses. They clinked the glasses. "What shall we drink to?" she asked.

"To beautiful women and love."

Flattering again, she thought. "And to handsome men and love," she added. "I have to ask you this," she said. "What are you looking for?" She knew she was nagging, but she could not help herself; she knew she was trying to break the spell, and then she would find out that—that what? *Omer is here, and it was a wonderful evening of good food, good wine, and pleasant company. He is clever and handsome, is a gentleman, and knows his way with women, so what is it he is looking for here with me?*

"I think I answered this question the first time we talked. I was married for four years, and we decided that was not a good choice. The differences were too vast to bridge, and we decided to split. Then the affair with the married woman. I do not feel like settling down at this time, but I want a relationship full of passion, understanding, and some mutual interests. I think this is something we can do together. What do you think?"

"And you have no problem with the age difference?" she said.

"Not at all," he said. "If you are concerned that I will be reluctant to be seen with you in public, this evening was proof to the contrary."

That was exactly what she was thinking of—that everyone could see that he was much younger than she. Then she realized she hadn't thought about it all evening. *What does that mean, Rey?* "Okay, I had to ask. Case closed."

Rey felt a bit tipsy. She liked to be light-headed; some of the voices in her head got quiet, and she felt relaxed and free-spirited. She got up, placed her glass on the table, took Omer's hand, and led him to the bedroom on the second floor. The room was dark, with only dim light coming from the ground floor and the streetlight outside the window.

Omer remained standing and waited while Rey took off her clothes. She left her black lace bra and panties on. Omer went close to her, turned her around, and kissed her neck. She felt goose bumps, and she turned and kissed him with a long, deep kiss, looking into his eyes. Omer got undressed and stood naked in front of her. Rey was afraid to look at him. He drew her close, took off her bra, and caressed her breasts, and they got in bed. He kissed her more and more. *How does he know that I love kissing so much?* she thought. "Omer," she whispered, "you need to know that I have not been with a man for a long time."

"I can feel that," he said. "Let me please you. Allow yourself to enjoy this, and we will advance at your pace. We are not going anywhere; there's no hurry. There is nothing more enticing than a woman enjoying herself."

CHAPTER

Eleven

⁂

REY OPENED HER EYES. It was three o'clock in the morning. Omer was lying next to her. When she moved, he opened his eyes. He touched her cheek gently and said, "How are you?"

Rey smiled. "Wonderful, and you?"

"Tired but content. No, just kidding. You really are something else, a real woman—ripe, sexy, sensual. A bit rusty, but sex is like riding a bike. With a bit of practice, it all comes back, and I am not going anywhere."

They talked some more and made love until dawn. Omer got in the shower. When he was finished, Rey handed him a towel and went downstairs to make coffee.

She was surprised things had gone so easily and naturally. She was not preoccupied with anything not related to the here and now—not with how her body looked, her breasts, or if she was too fat. Everything was simple, and the fact that she was a bit rusty did not make her uncomfortable. She felt how her body had come alive after being dormant for so long. Omer loved women and read them like an open book with no need for words. He appreciated them, respected them, and knew how to go about it. And his magic wand—well, that was a whole other story.

Omer came down to the kitchen and sat close to Rey. "Want something to eat?" she said. "Something sweet or a toast maybe?"

"No, thanks," he replied. "I don't eat in the mornings. Just coffee. I have a meeting in Jerusalem later, and they always serve the best of the best, and they don't take no for an answer." He finished his coffee, got up, kissed Rey lightly on her lips, and said, "I had a great time, just as I imagined, which leaves a taste for more. I am going now. I will call you later."

After Omer left, Rey remained seated by the table for quite a while, trying to understand what had happened to her in the last twenty-four hours. She'd done things she'd never dreamed she would dare to do. She'd gone out on a date with a much younger man without a hint of discomfort at being seen with him in public. She remembered David, a guy she'd liked very much when she was in her twenties. He was two years younger than she, and while they walked in the street, she was sure people were staring at her and rolling their eyes. Then there'd been Izzy, and now there was Omer, who was more than twenty years younger. However, despite that fact, she felt comfortable with him. Even while they were at the restaurant or on the street, she did not feel embarrassed or ill at ease. *This is incredible*, she thought. *It's all in the mind. Two people want to be together; they eat, drink, make love, talk, and enjoy themselves; and maybe they will even meet again. And everything is okay.* In fact, she was on cloud nine. Unfortunately, she had nobody to share it with.

She was out of touch with Batya, and Rey had never had a best friend she could tell everything to—maybe because Rey was not the type who talked about everything. Everybody thought of Rey as a happy-go-lucky, easygoing person who talked about everything, which was true, but there was a part of Rey that no one saw and none knew, except for Ronen. She'd met him at Batya's workshop. He was gay, and he was the closest thing to a best friend Rey had. She talked to him about things she could never talk to anyone else about, and he told her about his world and things about gay people. She learned firsthand, and it taught her a lot and made her understand and be emphatic.

However, Ronen had moved to Thailand, and now she had to process all of these exciting events in her life alone.

Omer called her late that afternoon. He asked her how she was and suggested they go to a movie. Rey was dying to see him. She wanted to say, "No movies. No nothing. Just come here and make love to me," but instead, she said, "Thanks, Omer, but my sister is coming over shortly, and we're going out."

That was not true, but Rey felt she needed some time for herself to digest what was happening to her. She figured she'd better go slowly. "Maybe tomorrow," she said. "If you want."

"Yes," he said, "I do want. Okay, pretty woman, have a nice evening with your sister, and call me after if you feel like it. You can call anytime."

"Okay," she said. "Thanks. Bye."

He hung up.

What if I fall in love with him? she thought. *That will be a disaster. He has everything to make this happen, and then I will die.*

Much to her surprise, her sister called shortly after.

"Hi, Rachel. What's up, Sis?"

"Are you busy tonight? You feel like going out?"

"No," Rey said, "I'm not busy, but I don't feel like going out. Why don't you come over here, and we'll catch up?"

"Okay," Rachel said. "I'll bring something with me. What do you fancy?"

"Oh, I don't mind. Whatever. Surprise me."

Rachel arrived after a short time with a bag full of stuff from the bakery. "Hey, Sis, what's going on with you? You look great. Did you have a facial?"

"No," replied Rey. "As a matter of fact, I have to see my facialist soon."

"Okay, so tell me—what did you have for lunch? I want that too. Your cheeks are rosy; your eyes are shining. You look like a million bucks."

Rey smiled. "Thanks, honey. It's always good to receive compliments." Rey brought out a plate and placed the stuff from the bakery on it. "You want coffee or wine?"

Rachel looked at her for a moment and said, "Wine is good, yeah. You don't need a reason to party, right?"

"Indeed," Rey replied. "So what's new and exciting in your life?" she asked.

"Oh, nothing much—work, home, home, work. Some friends. But what's up with you and the online excitements?"

"It's going okay," she said.

"Anything interesting lately? Any special talents?"

Rey said nothing. Rachel looked at her and said, "Oh, okay, I see. Now I understand the rosy cheeks and the bright eyes! So come out with it, Sis. Tell me all about it. Don't miss a thing."

"Nothing special," Rey said. "Just someone I met online, and we went yesterday to a restaurant in Jaffa."

"What! Who? From where? What does he do? How old is he?"

"He lives in Hod Hasharon, is a wine producer by profession, and studied in France, in the Bordeaux region."

"Yes, I'm listening," Rachel said. "What does he look like—a frog or a prince?"

"Neither," replied Rey. "He is good looking and very nice."

"Okay, and how old is he?"

"Oh," said Rey, "fortyish."

"Meaning?"

"He is thirty-eight," Rey said quietly.

"What! Wow, what is this? Are you completely out of your mind?"

"Rachel," Rey said assertively, "if you want me to ever share anything with you in the future, you will have to stop judging me. If you have an opinion on the subject, that's fine; I will hear it. Can we agree on that?"

Rachel looked at Rey for a moment. "Agreed. I'm sorry."

Rey told her only that they had gone to a restaurant, had a good time, and probably would meet again.

"Does he know how old you are?" Rachel asked, somewhat worried.

"My online profile states ten years less, so that's what he knows," Rey replied, "and he said that I look younger than my age."

"What is he looking for?" Rachel asked.

"Exactly what I am looking for: someone nice to be with, go out with, and have fun with."

"Okay, good luck to you, if that's what you want."

"Yes, that's exactly what I want at this time."

"Okay, keep me posted. Tell me how things are progressing."

Rachel left, and Rey took a deep breath. She did not need all of those comments from Rachel added to the anxieties she already had. *Que será, será.* Even if she and Omer did not meet again, she'd had a wonderful experience—exactly what the doctor had ordered.

Omer sent her a text message at about eleven o'clock that night.

"Are you awake?"

"Yes," she replied.

"Can I call you?"

She sent a smiley face.

Omer called. "Hey, what's up? How are you?"

"Fine, and you?"

"It's been a long day but a productive one. How did it go with your sister?"

"Well, we didn't go out after all. She came over, we had some wine and chatted a bit, and then she left. I think I will go to bed now. I'm tired."

"Okay, sweetie, just wanted to hear your voice and say good night."

"Good night, Omer."

"Thanks. We'll talk."

"Yes, definitely. We'll talk tomorrow."

She felt as if they had known each other for a while, and it scared her. They'd met two days ago. *And it feels like … what? Too nice, too easy, and too quick. Easy come, easy go,* she reminded herself.

She got in the shower, stood for a long time under the hot water, and then went straight to bed. She lay on her back and felt her body relaxing one muscle at a time, from her toes to the tip of her head. There was something sensual in letting the body relax like that. She felt calm and at peace, and she fell asleep immediately.

When she woke up the next morning, she couldn't remember the last time she'd had such deep, relaxed, good sleep. *Well, if that's what sex does to you, perhaps I should increase the dosage. Rey, darling, since when have you become so horny? Remember the Dahn Ben-Amotz book* Fucking Is Not Everything? *Well, yes, but I was seventeen then, and today*

I am a bit older, and I know that it's not everything, but it's a lot, especially if it's in the right pace and dosage. That's the thing.

She finally decided to stop the interpretations and speculations and enjoy the choice she'd made about Omer. She'd follow her instincts and ignore the chatter in her head telling her otherwise. What was the worst that could happen? She would have an enriching, pleasant experience to look back on, the kind she'd forgotten she could feel.

Omer called her regularly, and Rey could not ignore the feeling building up. She began expecting his calls, and she had someone in her life now who made her wake up in the morning with a smile. She felt a constant fear that the relationship would end sooner or later. She tried to live in the here and now and enjoy the moment.

They met during the week and on the weekends, went out, and traveled some. Rey started cooking again. She was motivated to show off her culinary skills, and she did it with great pleasure. Omer, the sommelier, was in charge of the wine.

Omer turned out to be a wonderful lover. He allowed Rey to proceed at her own pace, which was something she had not experienced before. She allowed Omer to lead her and totally gave in to her feelings; her discomfort was gone. Rey found in herself a side she had not known existed. She was full of passion and initiative, new traits that never had come to the surface until now.

Her phone rang; it was Omer. She noticed now that whenever she saw his name on the screen, she blushed. "Hello?"

"Hi. How are you?"

"Fine. How are you?"

"I am here in Jaffa in a meeting, and I have another meeting later, so I thought I'd come by for a few minutes if it's okay."

"Sure, of course."

"Okay then. I'll be over in fifteen to twenty minutes."

"Okay, I'll be waiting."

Rey felt her body coming alive just at the thought of Omer coming over. *He is coming just for a few minutes,* she told herself. *Don't start developing unreal expectations. And besides, what is it with you? You've become a sex addict? That's all you have on your mind lately.*

Get a grip, girl, said the other voice in her head. *How long have you been abstinent? I'm simply catching up.*

Her cell phone rang again. "Hi, Omer. What's up?" She was afraid he'd had a change of plans and was not coming after all.

"I'm on my way. I was delayed a bit, and I suddenly wanted to hear your voice."

"Really?" she replied, almost whispering.

"Rey, are you okay?"

"Yes," she said, "I was just thinking of you when you called."

There was silence, and then she heard him say softly, "Is what I hear true?"

She hesitated for a moment and then said yes.

"What is it? Tell me. It's okay. I'm on the same wavelength as you."

"I don't know. After you called and said you were coming over, suddenly, I wanted so much to be with you. It's a bit embarrassing," she said softly.

"That's what I feel too. Where are you? Where do you want me to be?"

She hesitated for a moment and then said, "Here with me."

"So open the door."

She went to the door and opened it. Omer was standing there. He came in, closed the door behind him, placed his cell phone on the table, took Rey in his arms, and kissed her strongly and passionately. Then he looked at her for a moment and said, "Rey, what are you doing to me? I am thinking about you all day; I can't get you out of my mind. My thoughts are constantly wandering to you. I can close my eyes and feel you and smell you."

Rey felt weakness in her knees. "You took the words out of my mouth," she said.

"I don't remember the last time my body reacted to a woman this way." He touched her body.

"What is this?" she said. "This constant desire. Wanting more and more." She whispered, "It's scary. Are these signs of sex addiction syndrome? Nymphomania?"

Omer looked at her and smiled. "My darling Rey, this is a syndrome of a woman healthy in body and soul, a woman full of passion and a will to live life to its fullest after a long period of dreariness. The next time you say a prayer, you should thank to whoever you pray to for the amazing gift given to you."

Rey kissed him and said, "Yes, you are right. I will certainly express my gratitude and count my blessings, especially this one—this gift and its wonderful wrapping."

Omer checked the time, picked up his cell phone, and started dialing. "I have another meeting, and I'm running late," he said. "Are we still on for tonight?"

"No, it's fine if we postpone this for tomorrow. The truth is, I'd prefer that too."

"Okay, tomorrow then. Same time, same place. Bye-bye."

A little while later, Rey was in the shower, when Omer knocked on the door and walked in. "Guess what? My meeting was postponed until tomorrow. Let's go celebrate."

They went to a small restaurant specializing in slow-cooked meat stews, red wine, charcuterie, salami, and dried-meat products. Omer parked his car, took Rey's arm, and started leading her toward the restaurant.

Suddenly, she heard a familiar voice. "Rey, is that you?"

She turned her head and saw Tammy and Yael. *Oh God, now the drilling starts, and I have no desire to share with them anything.* "Hey," she said. "What are you doing here?"

"That's exactly what we wanted to ask you," they said simultaneously, staring at Omer shamelessly.

Rey turned and said, "Girls, meet Omer. Omer, these are my friends Tammy and Yael."

They both said it was nice to meet him and shook his hand.

"We have just arrived," Omer said. "Rey has not been to this restaurant. I think it's excellent. You know the place?"

"No, we have not been here yet. We wanted to, but it's full," Yael said.

Omer looked at Rey for a moment and thought maybe he would try to talk to Gerard, the owner, but he saw Rey's look and finally said, "Yeah, it's a small place. You have to book a table in advance."

"Okay," said Tammy. "We'll try again. Enjoy."

"Thanks," Rey replied. "We'll talk."

"Was nice meeting you, Omer," Yael said, and Rey and Omer entered the restaurant.

CHAPTER

Twelve

⚜

Tammy called early the next morning. "Who is this hunk, Rey? You're hiding things from us? Not nice. I thought we were friends." She bombarded Rey right up front.

"I met him online a short while ago." She didn't volunteer any further information.

"Oh yes," Tammy said. "Did you make a profession change?"

"Meaning?"

"Caring for the very young?"

"Watch it, Tammy," Rey said. "Your claws are showing. Jealous?"

"Of course I'm jealous! Wouldn't you be?" Tammy was apologetic. "I would give ten years of my life for such a thing."

"Hey, don't get carried away. He is charming, and we are having a good time, at least for now."

"So tell me who, what, and where."

"He is thirty-eight, and he's a wine producer. We met online. We went out, and it was nice, so we met again. That's pretty much it."

"You know this can't be serious, right?"

"Tammy, my darling, who wants to get serious now? I want a mate who is good company, nice to be with, and interesting to talk to and to have sex like in the movies. And that's exactly what Omer is."

There was a moment of silence. "Wow," Tammy said, "seems you hit the jackpot. Good for you, girl. I salute you. You always had the courage. I wish you only the best; I want you to know that. Let everyone get green in the face with envy."

Friday morning, Omer called and asked Rey if she felt like going out to lunch somewhere. "I would love that," she replied. "Let's go to that place in Jaffa by the sea."

"Okay," Omer said, "we're on. I'll pick you up in half an hour if that's okay."

"Perfect," she said.

They ordered the same meals they'd had last time. Rey wanted fried squid, and Omer ordered the seafood platter in butter and garlic sauce. They shared a cold bottle of white wine. It was a beautiful, sunny day; the sea was flat; and people were walking on the beach. It felt like being on a beautiful island in the Caribbean. They ate, talked, and laughed. It was wonderful.

Toward the end of the meal, Omer placed his fork on the table and took Rey's hand in both of his, and for a moment, he was serious. "I received an offer to go to France for a few months to attend a series of workshops and tour some of the most prestigious wineries in France. About a year ago, one of the most important winery owners visited us here, and I accompanied him to wineries all over the country. He was quite impressed with the Israeli wine industry—and with me as well, it seems—and that is how the invitation transpired."

"So when are you leaving?" Rey asked.

"Well, I do not have a date yet, but probably in a few weeks."

"Are you excited?" she asked.

"Yes," he replied. "Very. This is a big compliment and quite a vote of confidence for me personally and professionally, and for me, it is an opportunity to learn from the top of the top in the industry, not to mention a significant upgrade for me as a wine producer."

"And the icing on the cake is," Rey said, "that all of this is taking place in France. Is there a better place to learn about wine? I am really happy for you."

"Yes," Omer said. "This was totally unexpected. I am in permanent contact with Jean Michel Marcier, and he did not even hint at his intentions. The old fox cooked up everything quietly. I got a call yesterday from the head office to inform me of this invitation. I needed twenty-four hours to digest all this."

So that's it, she thought. *It's over. Well, it's better this way than if he would have told me this is over because he's had it.*

"Rey, remember when we first talked on the phone, and you asked me about this thing I have with older women? And what did I tell you? That they are fun to be with."

"Right."

"And I also told you that if we spent time together, you would see that I was not trying to flatter you."

"Indeed," Rey said.

"And here you are, confirming my opinion about older women: wise, sensitive, clever, and fun to be with."

"Well, with someone like you, it was easy for me to express everything I have to give, even if it was a bit slow and rusty at first."

"Thanks for the compliment," he said.

"And thank you for the patience," she replied. They both burst into laughter.

CHAPTER
Thirteen

OMER WENT TO FRANCE. Rey thought about the wonderful time they'd had together, and she was amazed to find how grateful she was for the opportunity to feel like a woman again, to feel sexy and desired, and to have that kind of passion for a man. She realized she had discovered another side of her that she hadn't known existed. She did not fall apart with grief and go into depression when it ended. She was grateful for the opportunity, and she had followed her instincts and made the most of it.

They stayed in touch, and he shared with Rey in his long email messages the wonderful experience. She could practically taste and smell the wines, and she learned quite a bit in the process.

While Rey had been with Omer, she had not checked the dating website. She was not even curious to see who'd visited her profile, and even after Omer departed to France, she was still enjoying their episode, remembering all of the delicious moments. It had been wonderful, and now she was ready to continue on her journey, which she called "the road less traveled and beyond," after Scott Peck's book by that name.

After a while, she went back to checking the website to see what had been happening while she was gone. If she saw an old message from someone she thought was worth checking, she replied, "Sorry about the delayed reply. If it is still relevant, I would love to hear from you." She corresponded with some via the chat feature and on the phone. She connected with one guy who lived down south, and they talked for hours on the phone. He told her he'd been divorced for twenty years, but he still lived with his ex because he could not afford his own house, and they'd had another child together while being divorced. This was not someone she was contemplating even meeting. He was a perfect example of the saying "Why make it simple if you can make it complicated?" He wanted to meet her, but she said, "You are nice to talk to, but I don't think so." When he asked why, she replied, "You really want me to tell you?"

One day she received a message. He was forty-three, 1.85 meters tall, and well built, with green eyes. "I want to meet you," he wrote. "Please send me your phone number, and I'll call you." There was no photo. She saw that he was online and asked him if he was aware of the age difference between them. She could not help herself, as much as she tried to get rid of the habit.

He replied instantly, "Indeed. I love older, ripe women."

She sent her phone number, and he called immediately.

"Hi, Rey, it's Benny. You just sent me your number."

"Yes," she said.

"How are you?" he asked.

"Very well, thank you, and you?"

"I'm good, and I will be better after I meet you."

Okay, she thought, *this guy is not wasting his time.*

They talked a little. "Where do you live?" he asked. Rey told him.

"When can I see you?"

"Thursday?" Rey said.

"Thursday?" he said. "Today is Sunday, and I have to wait until Thursday? No way. I have to see you. You don't know what you are doing to me. Can I come now?"

What is it with this guy? she thought. "No," she said.

"So when?"

"Tuesday."

"Okay," he said.

"Tuesday afternoon. Is four o'clock okay?"

"Okay, see you then, woman."

Rey was already familiar with the various styles of conversations and what they meant, and she always enjoyed the compliments, especially the term *woman*. It had a special meaning for her—it was a confirmation that she was indeed becoming a woman again in the whole sense of the word.

There was something in Benny that triggered her, and she was curious to meet him. She felt she was confident and experienced enough to handle any situation.

Benny called on Tuesday to get her address, and he told her it should take him thirty to forty-five minutes to get there, depending on traffic. Rey gave him directions, and he said he would use his GPS. Rey decided it was showtime. She would make a grand entrance, so to speak. She put on her little black dress, thin transparent black pantyhose, and her black stilettos. She stood in front of the mirror, admiring her image, and said, "Mirror, mirror, on the wall, who's the sexiest of them all?"

Forty minutes later, he called again and said, "I'm lost." Rey gave him directions again, and he said, "See you in a few."

Rey looked out the window and saw a white four-wheel-drive BMW pull up in front of the house. The door opened, and a tall, well-built man in blue jeans, a black T-shirt, and Ray-Ban sunglasses got out. She stopped breathing. *This is the Greek god Apollo in the flesh who has come especially to see me.* She felt she was blushing all over, and excitement mixed with anxiety flooded her. *What if he doesn't like me? And he will come in, have a cup of coffee, make up an excuse, and leave.*

Rey, darling, said the other voice in her mind, *this is getting old, so get a grip and relax.*

He rang the doorbell, and Rey opened the door. He took off his sunglasses and kept standing at the entrance. His green-blue eyes checked her out. Rey felt as if he completely undressed her, and then he said, "Going somewhere?"

"Yes," she replied, "I have a blind date."

He hesitated for a moment, and to break the awkwardness, she said, "How did you get lost? I thought you said you have a GPS."

"Yes, I do, but don't you know that men don't need GPS to find an address?"

"Yes, right. I forgot. That's why Columbus reached America instead of India."

"Nice," he said. "Quick and sharp. I like that."

She invited him to come in, and he sat on the white couch. "Can I offer you something to drink?" she asked.

Benny did not answer. The way he looked at her, she knew he was in a completely different place.

She did not wait for his answer; she went to the kitchen and took out a wine bottle and an opener. Benny followed her to the kitchen, came up from behind, held her, and whispered in her ear, "The photo you have in your profile does not do you justice. It's not even close to the real woman. But do not change it for now. I don't want any competition."

Rey felt her heart jump out of her chest. She felt weakness in her knees and a flash of heat all over her body. She'd never had this kind of excitement toward someone she'd just met, a man who was a total stranger to her.

Rey poured the wine into two tall glasses, gave him one, took the other, and went into the living room. Benny placed his glass on the table, took her glass out of her hand, and set it down too. He walked over to Rey, strongly pulled her close to his chest, and kissed her hungrily. Rey felt his body harden, and excitement flooded her body.

"You know," he said, "that's exactly how I felt just from talking to you on the phone. I knew before I saw you."

Rey distanced herself from him, picked up her wine glass from the table, lifted it, and said, "To the surprises awaiting us." She felt she had to drink the wine in order to feel free and relax a little. This was all happening too fast, and the way she felt was unfamiliar to her.

Benny sat on the couch sideways, pulled Rey over, and started caressing her body. She felt dizzy. She was not sure if it was the wine or the passion. He asked her to get up and lifted her dress. Rey stood in front of him in her transparent black pantyhose with nothing underneath.

"Why don't you wear a G-string? On you, it would look crazy sexy." He pulled her over, kissed her through the pantyhose, and whispered, "You don't know what it feels like to do this." He turned her around, pulled down her hose, and opened his zipper. His magic wand was hard and ready. He took her hand and placed it on his erect penis. "Hold it. Feel it. You don't know what's going on here. This is crazy."

Rey thought she was going to faint. She felt flooded with currents and desire. Her heart raced. *If it does not happen now, I will die.* She felt her knees trembling and was almost not able to stand straight. Their encounter was quick, intense, and powerful, with an explosion and an aftershock.

Benny sat on the couch and pulled her to him. When she looked, his eyed were closed.

"Do you understand now what you did to me?" he said.

Yes, she thought, *and what you did to me—a volcanic eruption. Sex with clothes on, standing in stilettos—like a porn movie.* Rey poured herself some more wine.

Benny asked for some coffee. "I have to drive all the way back. I still have meetings today." He took out his cell phone and looked. "I have twenty-five unanswered calls," he said.

It was 6:20 p.m. He finished his coffee and said he had to go. She saw him to the door, and he kissed her neck and said, "You have an intoxicating body. I could start all over again, but I will leave now. I want to have this taste for more."

After Benny left, Rey sat for a long while, sipping the wine, still trying to understand what had happened. *How can it be?* she thought. *How is it possible for me to reach such powerful physical ecstasy with a man on the first date and allow myself to go all the way without feeling guilty, embarrassed, or uncomfortable?* What type of metamorphosis was she going through? Quietly, out of nowhere, another Rey had come out of hiding, a different Rey who was wild, bold, daring, and confident and allowed herself to try what was good for her and whatever suited her without having to answer to anyone but herself. As it happened, these were the kinds of men she chose. *If what he wants fits what you want, then by all means, go for it, girl, and only the best will do.* She lifted the glass of wine and said, "To your new other face, pretty woman. Cheers."

Chapter
Fourteen

Benny called after two days. He asked how she was and said he wanted to see her. He came late morning the next day. They sat and talked. He told her he was divorced and had a three-year-old boy who was very attached to him. He was the one who'd wanted to divorce; he'd suggested they have an open marriage, but she'd refused. It was hard for him to be away from his boy. He said he admired older women and connected easily with them, unlike young ones. He wanted to have more children and would probably get married again sometime but not now. Their first date, he said, was a powerful experience. He had a strong sex drive, which had been one of the difficulties in his marriage. "What you awoke in me," he said, "is something that has not happened to me in a long time."

This time, their sex was different; they took their time. There was no rush, even though Benny made her feel a much more intense desire than she'd ever experienced before.

He looked at her and said, "You have such an amazing body. Someone has to paint your body. This is a body of a woman."

Rey felt awkward. She did not think of her body as amazing; she thought her body was okay. She wanted, like most women, to shed a few pounds and tone her muscles. But if a sexy young man said she had an amazing body, why argue?

Benny got up and went to take a shower. He said he had to leave.

Rey understood. *This is going to be the ritual. He will come for a couple or three hours and leave.* She did not think they would become a couple, but she wanted something more than just the sex. She wanted an intellectual interaction. *Like they say, it's more important what a man has between his ears than between his legs. Really, Rey?* she asked herself. *Okay, both.*

The next time he called, Rey said she wanted them to have an evening together, and he agreed.

He came around seven o'clock. Rey prepared some snacks, cheese, and wine for them to nibble on. The atmosphere was pleasant, in spite of the fact that every encounter with Benny had sexual tension in the air.

After they made love, he checked his phone. "It's from home. I'll just return the call. I hope everything is okay."

He went to the balcony to get some privacy and returned after a few minutes. "It's my ex. The boy is crying and doesn't want to go to bed. He wants his daddy. I told him I was on the way." He got dressed and left.

Benny called the next day and apologized. He said he was sorry he'd had to go, and in the same breath, he asked if she would be available in the afternoon. He could come around three o'clock. Rey said she didn't know yet and would call him back later.

Toward the evening, she sent him a text message: "Benny, it seems that my wishes and your wishes do not coincide at this time. I want to thank you for this unique experience. Hope you find what you are looking for. Wish you well. Rey."

After she sent it, she read it a few more times and said to herself, *Rey, I am proud of you, and I like the way you have changed.*

Tammy called. "Hi, Rey. How have you been? You vanished into thin air. Did you discover the tree of knowledge and forget all about your friends?"

"No, Tammy, not at all. I have been busy with all these courses I have taken. I probably got carried away, but they were all so interesting I could not resist."

Rey chose not to share the episode with Benny; she was salivating just thinking of it. "But I have two weeks off now, so let's get together," she said.

"I was thinking," Tammy said, "maybe we could go down to Sinai for a few days. I could use the peace and quiet of the desert, beautiful sunrises, blue skies, and calm waters. If we go now, it will be before the season starts, and it will not be too crowded. We'll go down by bus and fly back. I don't feel like driving to Eilat and leaving my car at Taba. What do you think?"

"Sounds perfect," Rey said.

"Super," said Tammy. "I will book us the bus tickets. We'll leave at a reasonable hour—say, about ten o'clock in the morning. We'll be in Eilat by about three o'clock and continue on to Nueba."

"I have a book on Sinai with all types of accommodations, from five-star hotels to huts on the beach," Rey said. "They all have phone numbers to make reservations. Come to my place tonight, and we'll decide. What about Yael? Would she like to join us?"

"I don't think so. She has some unpleasant family business, but I'll ask her."

"Okay, I'll see you tonight."

They got together that same evening with the book, debating. "Five stars and Sinai don't go together; I tried it once," Rey said.

"Did you ever try a hut?" Tammy asked.

"No, I didn't," Rey replied, "but how about we try it? If we don't like it, we can always upgrade. Agreed?"

"Cool," Tammy said. "I like the idea of going into the unknown."

They called one of the places that had huts and other accommodations. "I love going down south by road," Tammy said. "There is magic in the slow, gradual entrance to the desert, especially south of Beer Sheba. I find the change of scenery and colors very primal and exotic."

The two of them spent the time on the long bus ride to Eilat catching up. Tammy told Rey she'd had it with men and dating and didn't know what she wanted anymore.

"But that is the most important thing," Rey said. "If you don't know what you're looking for, how will you find it? What do you want now?"

Tammy replied, "I don't know."

"You want to get married again?"

"Me? Are you nuts? No way."

"Okay, so you're not looking for a long-term relationship at this point. If you could have anything you want, what would you choose? What sort of a relationship? What is it you do want now?"

"Somebody nice," Tammy replied. "We should have some things in common, and we could meet once or twice a week to do things together, like go to the movies or travel together on the weekend—you know, be at ease with no pressure of any kind."

"What about sex?" Rey asked. "No sex in the package?"

"Yes, sure," Tammy said.

"Well, why didn't you mention it?"

"I'm a bit apprehensive. It's been awhile, and I forgot how this works," Tammy said, feeling a bit awkward.

Tammy had been divorced for ten years. She was fifty-eight and had a married daughter and a son attending university in the United States.

"Darling," Rey said, "it's exactly like riding a bicycle; it comes back to you, especially if it's important to you, and it's okay to tell your mate that it has been awhile. Someone who is mature enough will understand and will walk you through it at your pace."

Tammy looked at Rey and said, "You think so?"

"I know so. I have been there. It was not too long ago—did you forget?"

They reached Eilat and took a cab to Taba, the border terminal to Sinai and Egypt. They went through passport control and waited for transportation to Nueba. Someone pointed to a big van that had seen better days. The driver was a big Sudanese man wearing a long, dirty djellaba gown of unidentified color. He approached them and asked, "Nueba?"

They said yes. He wanted to take their bags, but they said they'd keep them on their laps. They'd seen him throw the other passengers' bags onto the van's roof and tie them with something that used to be a rope. Someone outside the van asked them for money, and he gave them a piece of paper written in Arabic that must have been a receipt. But who cared? There, the laws of the desert ruled.

They boarded the van and waited for the Sudanese to finish loading. Suddenly, a huge black foot appeared on the window, wearing a shabby sandal. It belonged to the Sudanese guy. It was not clear why he needed the sandals; it seemed his foot had a layer of dry skin thicker than his sandal. Perhaps they were a status symbol.

They hit the road. During the ride, it appeared the Sudanese driver's feet were not just padded but heavy too; he did not lift his foot from the gas pedal, not even on the road's curves. They decided not to think about what could happen with that driving style and told each other jokes, laughing all the way. When they reached Nueba, they told the driver the name of the accommodation they were heading for, and he showed them a trail he said they needed to take. It looked like the beginning of the trail the children of Israel had taken out of Egypt. After they insisted in Hebrew, Arabic, and English, he gave up and took them to their destination. As it happened, it was about two miles from the main road where he'd wanted to drop them off. *Well, the laws of the desert.*

They were greeted warmly at the site, which was called Kumkoom Talata. It seemed they were the only guests there. The bedouin host, Sammy, spoke good Hebrew and asked if they would prefer a room or a hut. They said they would take the hut, and if they decided otherwise, they would move into a room.

He said, "No problem," a phrase he used quite a bit. He took their bags and showed them to their hut. It was a straw hut with no door, and on the floor were some mattresses and what looked like stained wool blankets. They asked Sammy to remove the blankets since they had their own sleeping bags and asked if they could have some coffee. They also asked where the bathrooms were. He pointed toward something on a hill a short distance from the hut. It looked like ruins. They went to check the bathrooms and discovered the building had no doors or partitions. There was a toilet without a seat, as well as a twisted steel pipe used as a shower and a men's *pissoire*, or public toilet. Rey had brought a flashlight with her to use on her nightly trips to the bathroom. She hoped not to encounter someone like the Sudanese driver.

Then they went to the *zula*, an open space with a thatched roof facing the sea. The weather was perfect, and they felt the energetic vibe change to something soft, calm, slow, and pleasant. There were plenty of pillows placed on a bunch of carpets and back cushions. The two women sat down, and Sammy placed in front of them small coffee glasses and some cookies. "*Tfadalou. Al Ahsabi*," (Please enjoy. It's on me), he said

He asked if they would like to eat something, and they said no but wanted to know when dinner was served. He said, "Whenever you wish." They thanked him again.

"Five-star service in a straw-hut establishment," Tammy said. "For me, that's a first."

"This is wonderful," Rey said. "What a perfect idea. Who needs more? If I could imagine the Garden of Eden, this would be it. The combination of desert and sea, for me, is the ultimate impossibility—the colors, the peace, the pace of life here. There's no rush, infinite time, no radio, and no TV. I could easily build my dream home here."

"Yes," Tammy said. "Here, you don't die from a heart attack or high blood pressure, only from dysentery."

"You don't die here," said Rey. "You live in peace and harmony."

The days went by slowly and pleasantly. The Red Sea was a cure for body and soul. One day they went a bit farther from the zula. They took off their bathing suits and went into the water. It was a divine experience; the water caressed their nude bodies as they slowly entered. It was a pleasant, sensual, amazing feeling. They didn't feel like coming out of the water, and it became a daily ritual to swim in the nude in a different spot of abandoned beach.

In the next few days, Sammy hosted another couple of guests. They came with their car and left in the morning to travel in the area. They returned late and were hardly seen. A couple of Italian tourists then arrived from Sharem El-Sheik for a day's visit to swim with a female dolphin who'd adopted a bedouin from the Tarabin tribe and become a tourist attraction. The food was good; they had omelets in the morning, fresh fish at lunch, and *makluba,* spiced lamb stew with rice, in the evening. They were even offered shrimp, beer, and wine.

Rey realized she did not need the flashlight for her nightly bathroom trips because there was a full moon. Every night, the moon rose slowly above the Gulf of Sinai and reflected in the water, creating a sense of another place and time. They fell asleep at night to the sound of the sea water hugging the shore. They learned to take showers while the sun was shining; otherwise, no hot water was available, since the sun warmed the exposed water pipes. All in all, it was heaven, the perfect vacation. They wished they could stay longer, but duty called, and after a week, they sadly said goodbye to Sammy. It cost them three hundred New Israeli shekels—about ninety US dollars— each for the week, and they gave Sammy one hundred shekels each as a tip. He didn't know how to thank them enough. They promised to come back. Rey started thinking about retiring in Sinai.

Sammy called them a taxi, and because they still had time before the flight back to Tel Aviv, they decided to stroll in Eilat.

They went to the mall, looking for duty-free bargains. Rey bought her favorite perfume, Narciso Rodriguez, and Tammy bought a pair of high-heel imitation snakeskin shoes. They went down to the beach, bought a falafel, and sat on the sand to eat their lunch. They walked to the airport. The flight was due in an hour and a half, and there were quite a few people in line at the counters. Tammy approached Rey suddenly and said, "Look at that guy over there near the woman with the blue jeans and the yellow shirt."

"Tammy!" Rey said, surprised. "What happened? You woke up?"

"Yes, look. He is a hunk. Wow, what a good-looking guy. He passed by me earlier, and he had these gorgeous blue eyes."

"So go to him, and introduce yourself."

Tammy looked at Rey with her mouth open. "Are you crazy? You think for a minute that I would do something like that?"

"If you don't do it, you'll never get to meet him."

When they looked again, he was already gone, but the woman in blue jeans and a yellow shirt was still there.

"I'll try to check this out for you," Rey said, and she turned and walked in the direction of the woman.

"Rey, are you nuts? Where are you going? What are you doing?"

Rey approached the woman and said, "My friend there"— she pointed toward Tammy—"really fancies the guy you were talking to earlier, and I wanted to ask you if he is available and what his name is. By the way, I am Rey."

"I'm Nurit," said the woman in the yellow shirt, "and as for your question, yes, he is available now—divorced. His name is Razi. He is a freelance reporter who wanders all over the country. Google him. I think he hangs out on most of the social websites and uses that name."

"Thanks, Nurit. You may have just made a mitzvah."

"Sure," said Nurit, "no problem. He's a nice guy—a bit crazy but nice. Good luck."

Rey went back to Tammy, who was still standing with her mouth open, and said, "Okay, his name is Razi, he's divorced, he is a reporter in the north, and you can Google him."

"You are totally and completely crazy. I have always known that you are crazy, but to approach a stranger like that, when you didn't even know if she might be his wife or girlfriend?"

"Relax, Tammy. She would have had to say only 'He is not available; he is mine,' but she gave me all the info I asked for and her blessing too."

The flight left on time, and they landed at Tel Aviv's Dov Airport and took a cab. Tammy didn't stop talking about what Rey had done and how she tended to exaggerate and do crazy things.

"Tammy, do you want to meet the guy, or do you want to moan and groan? You said you liked him, so I went to find out for you who the man is. What happened?"

"So what now?" Tammy asked.

"Look him up on Google, and see what you find. He is a reporter; it should not be a problem. Then we'll see what we do next. And we're done for today."

At home, Tammy found a lead. From there, she found his blog on one of the websites. There were some photographs and a few posts. He had beautiful eyes and a penetrating, somewhat intimidating look. There was an option to send a message to his private email box.

"What should I write to him?" Tammy asked.

"What do you want?" replied Rey.

"To meet him," said Tammy.

"So that's what you're going to write to him. On social websites, you can offer to be his friend, and then you can go from there. Do you have a blog on the website?"

"Yes, but I have not been on there for a while, and the photo there is really scary."

"Okay, so go into your profile, freshen it up, and make sure everything is updated. Since you are older than him, knock off a few years from your age."

"And what if he does not reply or says he is not interested?"

"Then you'll have to look for someone else, my dear. These are the rules of the game. If you don't try, you don't know."

Tammy debated if she wanted to jump into the cold water. But what other option was there? If she did nothing, she would have nothing. "Okay, here it goes."

CHAPTER

Fifteen

TAMMY SENT A REQUEST for friendship to Razi's private email box. He confirmed the friendship request after three days but did not add anything else.

Okay, sweetie, Tammy said to herself, *it seems you are not going to make this easy for me, are you?*

Per Rey's advice, she waited a day and then wrote to him, telling him she'd read some of his posts and particularly liked the one about his meeting with the Dalai Lama. "That is a once-in-a-lifetime opportunity you had, and I would love to hear how it happened," she wrote.

Then she called Rey to tell her about the bold thing she'd done. "Never in my life did I hit on a man before. I keep thinking, *What if he doesn't respond or says, 'Thanks, but no thanks'?*"

"That's part of the whole thing here," said Rey. "There is no other way. Once, we used to run with the school crowd, then in the military, and then at work. Now we have the internet. It has its pros and cons. On the internet, you can go on a date in your pajamas, or without, and make an impression that you are Naomi Campbell. Instead of a first date, you can chat with a guy online, Skype, or simply talk on the phone and get an idea of who you're dealing with and whether or not you want to actually meet the guy—or you might already know this is not it. And yes, along the way, you will meet all kinds of people, including weirdos and freaks who will suggest you put a camera on your Skype, strip naked, and masturbate together. Everyone can pick and choose things to his or her liking. The first time it happened to me, I was in a state of shock. I don't have a camera on my computer, and I had no use for it. I said, 'Thanks, but no thanks,' and lived to tell about it. Not to mention he looked like the Hunchback of Notre Dame. Today, after the few first lines of correspondence, I can tell which way it is going. I learn every day."

Finally, Razi and Tammy started corresponding and chatting online.

Tammy felt he was sharp, sarcastic, and suspicious but interested. At times, he wrote things that Tammy felt had sexual insinuations, and she didn't quite know how to handle it. Rey suggested she check with herself what she wanted at that time and keep the conversation inviting but respectable. "Don't be tempted to use cheap language, dirty words, or graphic descriptions of any kind. Use words that will make him understand that you are indeed interested, if that is what you want."

It appeared Razi had a way with words—he was a reporter after all—but for some reason, he avoided phone conversations. Tammy did not disclose the fact that she'd seen him at the airport. She decided to save it for their meeting—if there would be one.

During one of their conversations, he told her he had a terrible backache and was really in bad shape and suffering. Nothing helped; painkillers gave him only short relief.

"Why don't you come take care of me?" he asked suddenly.

Tammy, who was an alternative medicine therapist specializing in Chinese medicine, ignored for a moment his invitation and said, "There are many other options besides painkillers, you know. Have you tried Chinese medicine therapy?"

"What is it?" he asked.

"It's a kind of alternative medicine. I will not bore you with the details, but I am a great believer and have seen many people who could breathe easier after a few of these treatments." It took a moment for her to absorb the fact that he had invited her to come over, and she decided she was going to take him up on it. "Well," she said, "if you will ask nicely, I may come to treat you." She felt her heart racing while waiting for Razi to reply.

"Are you serious?" he asked.

"Yes," she whispered.

"Okay," he said, "why not? It can't get worse. Let's give it a try."

Tammy called Rey. She was freaking out and in a total panic. "I went out of my mind completely," she said. "I don't know what happened to me." She told Rey what she'd done.

"Good for you, babe. I salute you and give you my blessings. Remember, do only what suits you and feels good; don't do anything because somebody expects you to."

Tammy boarded the 2:30 p.m. bus. She bought a one-way ticket. As for the return, she would decide when she was there.

Razi waited for her at the bus terminal, and they got into his car. It was a short distance to his house, and she didn't have a chance to examine him. They chatted for a bit, and after ten minutes, Razi parked the car in front of a seven-story building.

"How are you today?" she asked.

"A little better. I took quite a few pills today. I decided I am not taking any more of those, or they will ruin my liver. So keep your fingers crossed."

"If you want, I can give you a treatment now, on the house."

"Like what?"

"A bit of massage and acupuncture. We'll see what the situation is."

"Needles? No way."

"You decide," Tammy said pleasantly. "You are the one hurting."

"The needles—do they hurt?"

"Not at all. These are very thin needles—a quarter of a millimeter. You will hardly feel anything at all."

"Okay. I'll try, but if it hurts, I'll tell you, and we'll stop."

"Sure," Tammy replied. "Are you always this apprehensive?"

"Not always. Only when it has to do with needles." He paused and then asked, "Do you want to drink something?"

"Yes," she said. "I'd love a glass of cold white wine."

"And then you're going to stick me with the needles?"

"Don't worry, my dear. One glass of wine is good to relax and be focused. If you're hurting, tell me where the wine is, and I'll help myself," Tammy said.

He walked to the fridge, pulled out a bottle of white wine, took two glasses from the cupboard, and placed them on the coffee table in the living room. "Pour one for yourself," he said. "I may have one later."

"I think a glass of wine will help you relax your muscles; it helps the treatment and speeds recovery."

Tammy poured wine into both glasses. She moved the wine in the glass, brought it close to her nose, and savored the aroma of the wine.

Razi looked at her and smiled. "Very nice. You are some kind of a connoisseur? Someone who understands wines?"

"Not really," she said, "but I like the ritual of using all five senses. That is why people clink the wine glasses—to use the sense of hearing as well." Tammy took one sip and then another. Razi took a small sip and placed the glass on the table.

He got up, took off his pants, and stayed in his underpants. He looked at Tammy for a moment and said, "We have hardly met, and you've already made me undress. You are really something else."

Tammy smiled and thought she'd scored two points for her initiative, creativity, and, most of all, courage. She got up, took out her treatment kit, and asked Razi to lie on his belly, relax his body, and close his eyes.

Razi, still kidding, said, "You are not going to do anything I don't want, right?"

"Ha-ha," said Tammy, and she thought, *The guy is really in a state of anxiety.* "Don't worry," she said. "Whatever I do, I'll be gentle." She placed her hand on his back, a bit above the tailbone, and immediately felt the tension in his body. She swayed his body a little and then placed her two hands.

"Mmm," he said. "Your hands are warm. It feels nice."

Tammy pressed and massaged a few points and asked, "Does it hurt?"

"No," Razi said, "not at the moment. The touch of your warm hands really feels good."

After a few moments of pressing and massaging, she felt the muscles become more relaxed. She took out the needles and started inserting them one by one. Once she'd finished, she heard Razi say, "Tell me before you start with the needles, so I can prepare myself."

"Okay," Tammy said, laughing.

"Why are you laughing? Did I say something funny?"

"I already inserted the needles a few moments ago."

"No, I don't believe you."

"Well, it's true. I told you it would not hurt. I hope this helps you be more of a believer."

Razi tried to turn his head and look at his back, but Tammy said, "Ah-ah-ah, no. Put your head down, and relax your back like before, please."

"Yes, ma'am."

After about twenty minutes, Tammy started pulling the needles out. She gently rubbed each spot, massaged the whole area, and placed her hands on Razi's back. Razi's eyes were closed; he lay motionless. Tammy thought he might have fallen asleep, but then he said, "Tammy, I could definitely get used to this."

"Stay like this for another ten minutes, and then slowly turn around, try to sit, and pay attention to how your back feels."

Razi did as she'd said. He sat on the couch, lowered his feet to the floor, and said, "It's much better. I do not feel any pain now, but it's probably because I was resting. We'll see how I feel in a few minutes after I get up."

Tammy filled her glass with more wine and took another sip.

"If you want to take a shower," he said, "the bathroom is straight back on the right, and there is another bedroom on the left. The fact that you came to my house does not commit you to anything."

Tammy smiled and said, "Spoken like a true gentleman."

"And in the bathroom, you'll find clean towels," he added.

When she got up, Tammy felt a little light-headed and tired from the long trip, the excitement, and the anticipation of what was still to come. She took her bag and walked toward the bathroom. Razi's bedroom was dark; only the hallway lamp provided some light. The room looked relatively tidy. There was a scent of laundry softener in the air. *He changed the sheets,* she thought. *That means he has some expectations.* Out of the corner of her eye, she saw Razi moving around the house. "Well, how are you feeling now?" she asked.

Razi walked into the room and said, "Listen, I don't believe in all this nonsense, but to be honest, I think the pain has almost totally disappeared."

Tammy smiled. "Try for a minute standing with your legs straight, and move your body, from the waist up, slowly and gently to the right and then to the left."

Razi did as she'd said.

"How does it feel?" she asked.

"It feels a bit tender, but there is no pain."

"Okay, great. Now try bending, keeping your legs straight and your hands hanging on the sides—slowly and gently."

"No pain at all," he said. "It's hard for me to believe. Can I give you a grateful, friendly hug?"

"Sure," she replied.

Razi approached her, gave her a hug, and then pulled back a little and looked at her. He kissed her lightly on her lips. Tammy closed her eyes and surrendered to her feelings. Razi kissed her again. This time, it was a long, sensual kiss. Tammy felt warmth filling her body. She had almost forgotten what it felt like to be desired.

"I want to take a shower," she said, and she went into the bathroom and closed the door. She took off her clothes and stood under the hot water flowing on her body. It was pleasant and caressing. She washed away all of the fears and anxieties and thought, *Tammy, you did it, girl, with flying colors. From here on, the sky is the limit.*

When she got out of the shower, she realized she had not brought fresh clothes to wear. *What do you need the clothes for?* said a voice in her head. *Going out somewhere?* She stood in front of the big mirror, which was partly covered with steam that blurred her image. She wrapped the towel around her body and said softly, "Okay, babe, it's showtime, the moment of truth." She opened the bathroom door and came out.

Razi approached with a glass of wine in his hand. "Want some?"

"Yeah, but just a sip. I already had some—too much on an empty stomach."

"Are you insinuating I have not offered you anything to eat?"

"No, not at all. I am not hungry," she said.

Razi gave her the glass, and she took a sip. It was an awkward situation. She was standing in the dark bedroom of a man she'd just met, wrapped in a towel, holding a glass of wine in her hand. What did that mean? It meant he really turned her on, and she was going for it.

Tammy handed Razi the wine glass, and he placed it on the nightstand. He approached her and took her hand that was holding the towel, and the towel fell to the floor. Tammy stood completely naked and was surprised to realize she was not at all embarrassed or uncomfortable; it even felt natural. Razi kissed her neck and shoulders while his hands caressed her body. She felt dizzy. "Razi," she said, "it has been awhile since my last time."

"It's okay," he said.

They got into bed. The sheets were cool and fragrant, and she felt ready to make love again.

Chapter

Sixteen

It had been quite awhile since Tammy had slept in a bed that was not her own with another person. She woke up a few times during the night, and it took her a moment to remember where she was.

It was six thirty in the morning, and Razi was still asleep. She sneaked out of bed, washed her face, and brushed her teeth. She looked in the mirror. It had been some time since she'd paid attention to how she looked in the morning. "My dear girl," she said to the image in the mirror, "not bad at all."

She went back to the bedroom, looking for her clothes.

"Good morning, Tammy," Razi said, and she turned her head. "Hey, how did you sleep?"

"Okay," she said, "considering."

"Meaning?"

"Not sleeping in my own bed and with someone else."

"Yeah," he replied, "I know what you mean. I want to tell you that I would have never guessed you were fifty-eight. Wherever I look, you really look like a million bucks. Honest."

"Thanks," she said.

"What made you decide to disclose your age?" he asked.

"Well, once we met, I felt it was appropriate. Tell me the truth, Razi. If you would have known how old I was before we met, do you think you would have asked me to come?"

"I don't know what to tell you. I think probably not. But it's interesting. This has probably been a positive discrimination. Lately, all my dates were much younger than me, and I found it to be quite tiresome. Specifically, they wanted to know if our relationship was becoming serious. I was married, I have two grown children, I was in a long relationship that ended about eighteen months ago, and I don't want any commitment at this time in my life—at least I don't want to declare it. If it happens, fine."

"I agree," said Tammy, "and also maybe to freshen up any fixed ideas you may have, don't you think? By the way, how is your back?"

"My back? Wow, I'd totally forgotten about it. How about that?"

"I suggest you handle your back gently for the next few days—no sudden motions. When you bend, bend your knees too, and do not lift anything heavy."

"Listen," Razi said, "yesterday I decided that if you succeeded in healing my pain, I would write an article in the form of an interview about you in my magazine. What do you think?"

"Great," Tammy said. "I could use a little publicity."

"Good. So we'll have breakfast, and we'll get to work."

Tammy gave him some background, professional history, and success stories.

"Okay," he said, "I will finish up later, edit it, and send it to you by email so you can review and approve. I assume it will be not in the next edition but the one after."

"That's great," she said. "Thank you."

"I will also write what my personal opinion was about this sort of treatment before and after."

Tammy smiled. "Before and after what? Some may say that you are biased."

"And they will be right. I have experienced you personally in both senses."

"Exactly," she said. "I hope they will not think that is a part of the treatment."

They both laughed.

Tammy called the airline to find out their schedule and booked a seat on the 2:00 p.m. flight to Dov Airport in Tel Aviv. Her cell phone was on quiet mode, as she'd decided to disconnect from the world, and when she turned the sound back on, she discovered Rey had sent her a text message asking if everything was okay, and one of her clients had called. Razi was in the shower, so she called Rey and said, "I am at Razi's house. Everything is fine. I'll be on the two o'clock flight to Tel Aviv. I'll call you when I get there."

Rey said, "Yahoo! Hallelujah! Are we going out to celebrate tonight?"

"Sure," said Tammy. "Quite a reason to celebrate. I lost my virginity—again. Ha-ha. Bye."

Razi came out of his room. He was dressed and said, "I have to stop at the office for a moment, and then we'll go sit somewhere by the sea."

"Shall I wait here?"

"No, come with me. It will only take a few minutes, and then we'll go."

They left the apartment and got into the elevator. The lift stopped at one of the floors, and a young woman got in. "Hi, Razi. How are you doing?" she said.

"Great. How about you?"

"I'm good."

"This is Tammy, a friend. Tammy, this is Nirit, my neighbor."

"Nice to meet you," Tammy said.

"Likewise," said Nirit.

Nice, Tammy thought. *He is a real nice guy and polite.*

They stopped at Razi's office, and Tammy waited at the reception while Razi went in. He returned after about ten minutes. "Come," he said. "Let's go sit in a nice place."

They sat and talked, and Razi told her about his days as a wild young reporter, his ex, his children, and his mother. Tammy listened with much interest. Then Razi took her to the airport. "Thank you for the devoted care," he said.

"For a second treatment, you will have to come to my clinic," she said. "Hope I helped."

"You bet," Razi said. "I really feel great now, and it was fun too. Have a pleasant flight. I'll mail you the interview's draft."

Tammy kissed his cheek, grabbed her bag, and disappeared inside the terminal. During the flight back, Tammy checked in with herself about how she felt, and to her surprise, she felt great. She felt she had passed this test with flying colors. The experience had been exciting and pleasant, and she'd had sex. She'd almost forgotten what it felt like. Yes, she'd done it, and she could do it and anything else she felt like whenever she felt like it. "Yahoo!" she wanted to scream. "Yes, I can!"

After she landed in Tel Aviv, she called Rey and told her everything that had happened.

"I'm proud of you, Tammy. You are something else, and you know that now. You are on the right path for a relationship with Razi or someone else. You did it."

Two days later, Tammy received an email from Razi. The draft was honest and flattering. Razi told about his personal experience and his skepticism about alternative treatments, and he said he had changed his mind now. He introduced Tammy and described her as "a charming fifty-eight-year-old woman."

Tammy didn't see the rest. "How dare he disclose my age!" she fumed. "Without asking for my permission or even mentioning the fact that he was going to write it!" She was in a state of rage as she dialed Razi's number.

"Hey, Tammy, what's up?"

"Razi, what on God's green earth made you put my age in your report without even telling me?"

Razi was silent for a moment. "That is why this is called a draft—so I can hear the comments," he finally said. "Besides, why do you object to me mentioning your age?"

"Because," she said, "it's irrelevant. What does my age have to do with anything?"

"Tammy, are you ashamed? Does it make you uncomfortable that people know your age?"

"No, what makes you think that? But I don't see a reason to advertise that either."

"What makes you so uncomfortable? You're fifty-eight, and you look forty-five. In bed, like thirty-five, and you have a soul of twenty-five, so what is there to be uncomfortable about? If I were in your shoes, I would place a sign on my back, reading, 'I'm fifty-eight. Ask me how I do it.' But, sweetie, I will write whatever you want. I just thought you wanted to hear my opinion on the subject."

Tammy called Rey and told her about the conversation she'd had with Razi.

"You know, Tammy, I think Razi is right, and I also think the trip to Eilat was worth it, even if it was just to hear this. You are lucky."

CHAPTER
Seventeen

SATURDAY AFTERNOON, REY WAS sitting on her beautiful porch, surrounded by flowerpots, shrubs, and various green plants. She was drinking a gin and tonic from a tall, sweating glass, one of which she kept in the freezer. She planned to spend the long afternoon slowing the pace and relaxing.

Her cell phone signaled a text message coming in. It read, "I met Ron at the Tel Aviv Port Café today, Saturday, February 14, Valentine's Day. He gave me your phone number. I would like to apologize for the way we parted and ask your forgiveness. I would have called sooner if I hadn't been too ashamed. Batya." Rey read the message one more time and placed the phone on the table. Batya had broken all ties with Rey abruptly without any explanation and in the weirdest way. Rey did not understand what had happened. She felt deeply hurt and could not make any sense of this. She decided to let it be. It was difficult for her, as Batya was her teacher at the workshop and her mentor. Rey consulted her on many issues in her life. They were not the best of friends, but they had a special friendship. Rey did not hold a grudge or feel any animosity toward Batya for the breakup, but she felt deep sorrow, especially during this time in her life, which was full of ups and downs. After hesitating for a while, she picked up her cell phone and texted back, "Forgiven."

Batya wrote her back almost immediately: "Thank you. This does not go without saying: I'd love it if we could get together."

"I will be in touch," Rey replied.

"Okay, thanks again," Batya wrote. "Have a nice day." It seemed life was full of surprises.

Rey and Batya met, and Batya told her what had happened during the time they'd been out of touch. Rey filled Batya in as well. There was something pleasant in their reunion; the bond between them got stronger, and they became best friends, not a teacher and a student anymore. However, Batya would always be Rey's spiritual mentor, and despite the fact that Batya was much younger than Rey, Rey felt she could tell her anything. Rey never had had a close friend, not even as a little girl or a teenager. It was strange. She thought, *I seem to be a late bloomer in many aspects, doing things now that most people do at a much younger age.* She recalled what Batya used to say: "There is no time in the cosmos."

Rey had to leave her job; she was told she'd reached her retirement age. Rey was mad at her boss. *What kind of bull is this?* She was not a government employee. She knew those employees were forced to retire. *I have not been working here for a million years, just three and a half, so what is this all about?*

But in life, as usual, things changed. There was a new management team, and they moved the company offices. Employees left, and the magic and wonderful atmosphere she'd experienced when she'd first started working there changed completely. She worked in an art gallery for a short period of time, worked for a bit in marketing, and did some coaching and volunteer work. All in all, she was quite busy. She learned a lot about computers. She was not quite a high-tech expert, but she improved rapidly due to the everyday need and the desire she had to learn and know more about that aspect of life, one that people could not do without anymore. Computers were the open communication channel to the world. It was pretty amazing. She tried to recall how the world had functioned before the internet era. She remembered buying her first computer—because people had told her she had to have one—and opening her first email. She had not been able to figure out who all of these people sending her messages were. *I don't know any of these people. Who are they?* she wondered. A friend told her the messages were junk mail. "What is junk mail?" she asked.

Now, when she was doing a crossword puzzle, she Googled for help. She used the internet to find addresses, check her bank account, and check the weather forecast. It was amazing, not to mention shopping online at one of the biggest department stores in the world: eBay. She had already figured out that in life, where there was a will, there was a way. *I can do whatever I set my mind to do.*

Rey spent much time in front of the screen. She covered a lot of material on the various websites, and while surfing, she reached many places where she found interesting stuff. Many social websites were not dating websites per se, but she discovered that wherever there were people, there was dating. On one of the forums, she met Israel. The forum's topic was relationships, which always generated interest. At one point, he asked if he could contact her outside of the forum. They exchanged email addresses and started to correspond.

He was forty-three years old; was a farmer; was married; had three children; and lived in a moshav, an agricultural settlement, up north. Rey loved his descriptive language and his connection to the land. Their correspondence went on for a few weeks. She found it pleasant that his emails were written at all kinds of odd hours. Eventually, they talked on the phone, and he said, "I have to meet you. You really intrigue me."

"What for?" she said. "It's nice and pleasant this way. You live miles away. Why would we want to get into a complicated situation?"

"I'll tell you something, Rey, and please treat this seriously. I do not lie, and I'm not trying to beautify things. In the last two years, my wife and I hardly talk to each other. Yes, we live in the same house—in separate rooms."

Yes, she wanted to say, *sounds familiar.*

"I don't know what is going to happen. She does not work, and I am in no position economically to leave the house and pay for two households. I will not bore you with the details. The truth is, I've never had an extramarital relationship, and this is the first time I am making a step in such a direction. I really want to meet you."

Okay, she thought, *what could happen? I'll see him once and see what happens.*

"It is a three-hour drive," he said. "I would like to leave early to avoid getting stuck in traffic. Would it be okay with you if I get there at about eight thirty or nine o'clock in the morning?"

"Yes," she replied. "Would you like a croissant or *borekitas*?" she asked, referring to the Greek-style pastry.

"Can I have one of each?"

"Sure," she said.

"Okay, we're on."

Rey did not see Israel's photograph, and he did not see hers. When he arrived, he rang the intercom, and she gave him her apartment number. When she heard his footsteps, she opened the door.

"Hi. Nice to meet you," he said.

"Same here," she said.

It was weird that people could create a nice, comfortable, flowing relationship on the phone or by email, but when they met in person, suddenly, they didn't know what to say. He was taller than she, and he had a shaved head (which he lost a point for), pierced ears, and an Indian head tattoo on his left arm (which he gained three points for). Rey loved men with pierced ears and tattoos—in the right dosage. She hated shaved heads. *Well, no one is perfect*, she thought. She asked him to sit down and went to make some coffee and get over the awkward moment.

Physically, he was not exactly her type. He was well built, with olive skin and big brown eyes. His hands were farmer's hands—she could see that—but they were clean and groomed. She also liked his perfume. They sat and talked. She asked him about the tattoo, and he said he'd gotten it while he was visiting the United States. He loved the Indian culture.

"I love the Indian culture too," she said. "And what is this thing with the shaved head?" she asked outright without hesitation. "I know it's the in thing now, this metrosexual male."

"Oh no," he said, "not at all. It's quite convenient, especially in my type of work. Yes, it's cold in winter, and I have a special woolen snow cap to keep me warm, and in summer, I wear an Aussie cowboy hat. Besides, you know what they say: 'God created so many clever heads, and the rest he covered with hair.'"

"Nice," she said. "I love it. Want some breakfast?"

He said he was too excited to eat and added, "Maybe later."

Rey took the empty coffee cups to the kitchen. She wasn't sure what to do next. What did she want? Israel followed her to the kitchen and said, "I'm dying to kiss you. Can I?"

"What? It's the first time we've met," she said, and she was immediately sorry for the stupid remark.

He did not lose his cool and just said, Okay." He went to the front door, opened it, went out, and closed it behind him. Then he opened it, walked in, and said, "How about on the second time?" They both burst into laughter.

This time, he approached her, took her in his arms, and kissed her. He opened his eyes, looked at her, and kissed her again, and then they went up to her bedroom. It seemed that in spite of the harsh reality Israel lived in, he was an attentive, patient, and gentle lover with a rare ability to postpone gratification. Rey felt his craving and need for intimacy, and she liked it.

Afterward, they prepared brunch from whatever they found available. Rey opened a bottle of wine, and they made a toast. Israel smiled, and his eyes were shining. "You know," he said, "when I left this morning, I thought to myself, *I am going to drive for three hours now to see a woman, and I have no idea what she looks like, and she is much older than me.* But when we talked on the phone, I liked you so much, and I am so glad I decided to come."

"Yes," she replied, "me too."

Israel left in the early afternoon so he could get home before rush hour. He called from the road and told Rey he'd had a wonderful time and really liked her. His visits turned into a once-a-week ritual. Israel arrived in the morning and left early in the afternoon. Rey cooked all kinds of delicacies, and they stayed at home for most of the day, eating, drinking, making love, and talking. She loved the early morning emails he sent her the morning after. One said,

> The drive back was smooth and easy. I feel like I am floating in the air on cloud nine. I receive so much from you, and it's amazing. The more you are relaxed and at ease, allowing yourself to receive, I feel stimulated, and all of my senses are awakened. So don't worry; everything is cool, and by the way, the eggplants you made were out of this world.
>
> From the man and the eggplant.

She liked the fact that he was so connected to the land, and she was moved by his descriptions:

> Delighted to read your words, words that are like raindrops on a burning body, words that are a cool breeze on a hot day. I am moved to read your reactions and have pleasure in our relationship, which, to me, is like earth and wind. Mmm, something to think about.

The connection between them was the result of a deep need for both of them. Israel, supposedly a family man, was a stranger within his own family. He was trapped in his own home and functioning as the family ATM card. He left at four o'clock in the morning for work, returned home in the evening, took a shower, had dinner, had some interaction with the kids, watched the news, and dove into bed. Rey noticed the yearning they both had for being together, for someone to love; the anticipation for their daily phone conversations, when they shared everyday small talk; and their yearning for their intense weekly rendezvous. Israel seemed like a simple man. He was a farmer who worked and loved the land. He could describe in an amazing way how the fields looked with first light, the smell in the air, the dewdrops on the wildflowers, the combine's dance with ears of grain, and the cranes in flight, looking for grain pickings and worms. He knew which animals were active in the various hours of the day and could describe the gradual change in the colors of the sky during and after sunrise, the shift in the direction of the winds during the odd hours of the day, and how all of it made him feel. "Man and nature," he called it. Outside with Mother Nature, he never felt lonely. He felt loneliness when he reached his home.

Israel had a unique sensitivity and a unique ability to observe everything that had to do with Rey. He found in her a friend, a lover, and a confidante. It took time for him to trust and open up to her, and with her, he dared to say things he'd never said out loud or shared with another soul. He also had infinite desire for her. He said he could not remember his body ever reacting to a woman that way, and he managed, with his infinite patience and skills, to take her to places she had never been before. He read her like an open book, and Rey taught him to express his own feelings and tell her what he wanted her to do. She loved to listen to him enjoying himself with her. He had sensuous lips, and his kisses sent strong currents throughout her body and made her dizzy. Sometimes she would wake up early in the morning; close her eyes; and imagine him touching her, kissing her, and murmuring things. She could get carried away and have an orgasm just from the thought. His emails filled a void and were some kind of a compensation for the time they spent apart. In one of his emails, he wrote,

Good evening, my woman. I've just gotten in after a hot, crazy day, and what a delight to find your email, which put me, in an instant, close to you, your lips, your eyes, and everything we have. Many times, I feel you are near me. It's crazy, but I have no problem doing that; I can bring you anytime. I hope your days are cooler and more pleasant.

From the man who views you as his shade in these hot days.

In another email, he wrote,

Good morning to you. You can't even imagine how I love reading your emails, which open a window to other worlds, to places I rarely go, and for that, I thank you from the bottom of my heart. At times, you come alive in front of my eyes, even if it's just for a moment. This weekend, I will be very close to you but so far away, so if you feel a brush of my lips, a whisper in the wind, or a slight touch, that's me so close to you and hell, so far away. Me.

The man who sees you when he first opens his eyes and again before he closes them at night.

Every now and then, she thought, *What if …*

Israel was much younger than she and was in an impossible family situation. Despite the fact that he and his wife were estranged, physically and mentally, he felt trapped. He didn't believe he could economically survive if he left the house because besides his job, he had no other financial resources or financial help. That made him feel like a married man, and he was wary about anyone finding out about his affair. There were times when Rey did not know until the last moment whether he would make his weekly visit. He told her once that his dream was to buy a farm down south, grow olive trees, raise goats, and produce cheese. "Would you come with me if I did?" he asked her once.

Rey recalled that after their third date, she decided to reveal to him her real age. "You know," she said, "there is something I told you about myself that is not accurate."

"What is it?" he asked.

"My age," she replied.

"I don't remember what you told me, and besides, what difference does it make? I saw you, I like you, and it would not change anything, even if you tell me you are one hundred years old."

"Yes," she replied finally to his question about the farm, "there are so many things you can do in remote places. You don't have the variety of possibilities the city offers, but it could be a unique advantage to have workshops, women's circles, and coaching and live close to nature." She could soar on the wings of her imagination and see herself in a simple wood cabin with carpets, a fireplace, and a brick oven filling the house with the smell of baking bread. The neighbors would live far enough away for her to have peace and privacy but close enough to come over for a visit and a meal. She liked the idea, but at the same time, she acknowledged the fact that she could easily get carried away. She knew that she and Israel lived in a sort of bubble, detached from reality. That was not the real world. She knew only a part of him; she had no idea how he dealt with everyday challenges and solved problems, and she did not know how she would adjust to living in a close relationship after being single for so many years. She could come and go as she pleased without having to answer to anyone, and she cooked and cleaned if she felt like it. If she didn't feel like it, she could leave everything lying around in a mess. She was the ultimate decision maker and determined what her priorities were. Rey knew that once she found her mate for a long-term relationship, she would have to make the necessary adjustments, and she had no problem with that. On the contrary, she knew that today, she was older, wiser, and ready; she just had to have the will, and the relationship had to be worth it. It had to be for the soul—no compromises.

Rey was strong-willed and courageous and had the ability to adjust to changes. People could like her or not like her, but they couldn't ignore her, and she knew that when the time came, she would be able to rise to the occasion and do whatever it took to make it work. She had no doubt about that. That was exactly what had happened with Mike.

CHAPTER

Eighteen

REY WONDERED AT TIMES if what she felt for Israel was love. She could not say for sure. The truth was, she had forgotten what it felt like to be in love.

She used to think she would be able to go to bed only with a man she was in love with; it would have been impossible otherwise. That was how women of Rey's generation were programmed: women slept only with the ones they loved, and the ones who did not behave, those who gave themselves easily, didn't deserve to be loved. *What did they call Ziva when she was in the army? The guys' mattress.* But now, after she had allowed herself to feel passion, be desired just because, and be okay with it, she could not tell whether what she felt for Israel was love. This was something completely new to her.

She quit visiting the dating websites, at least for now. Like Rey, Israel loved to eat and enjoyed good food, and he also enjoyed drinking. On the days when they were together, Rey prepared drinks, gin or vodka tonics, and they always had wine with lunch. Once, she gave Israel a taste of her homemade

Limoncello. "Wow," he said. "This is strong. It's good but really strong."

"Darling," she said, "this is made with ninety-six percent pure alcohol. The rest is sugar syrup and lemons."

He looked at her for a moment, and after he managed to get over the strong alcohol, he said, "You drink like a Cossack from the Ural Mountains."

They both laughed. "I love that," she said. "I would like you to come over for a weekend," she added. "What do you think?"

Israel looked at her and said, "I would love to do that very much."

She waited for the *but*.

"But I don't know how I can do that."

"What is the problem?" she asked.

"I can't disappear for a whole weekend without an explanation."

"You can say you are going to visit friends, which, by the way, is not a lie." She saw him shrinking in discomfort. "Would you like us to have a weekend together?"

"What kind of a question is that? Of course I want to."

"Then I think you have to get used to the idea first. My birthday is coming up in a few weeks, and it falls on a weekend. Come on Thursday night or Friday morning. What do you think?"

"Okay, we'll see."

For the following couple of weeks, Rey did not bring up the subject, and then, when they were on the phone one day, she asked, "Did you give some more thought to our weekend together?"

"Yes, I want that very much, Rey. I really do."

"Okay, and?"

"It's difficult for me," he said finally.

"You want to share it with me? Maybe two thinking heads can come up with something."

"The truth is, since I got married, I do not have any close friends, really."

"Do you do your periodic reserve military duty?"

"Yes," he said.

"So some of the guys there invited you to join a four-by-four desert tour. Very simple."

"Okay, it is a possibility. Let me work on it."

"Okay, great," she said. "I trust you can do that."

Israel's way of handling difficult situations was not to deal with them. Rey had already noticed that, but she'd never said anything; she'd had no need so far. *That is the thing*, she thought, *when you live in a bubble. You can leave the unpleasant things outside, until it is impossible when the problem penetrates the bubble.* She decided to let it be for now, until it was time. He chose not to share whatever he was doing or not doing, but she knew he would have to deal with it eventually—or not. When her birthday weekend approached, he said that he'd told his family about the desert trip, and his wife had raised an eye brow.

"Why?" Rey asked.

"Because it's unusual for me," he said. "I don't usually go out with friends to have fun."

"Well," Rey said, "it's about bloody time."

Israel arrived on Friday morning, later than usual, and looked stressed out. Rey greeted him with a long kiss and felt him relax a bit. "How was your trip?" she asked

"Trip was fine. Not too much traffic."

"Do you feel like going out for breakfast at Leon's? He has the best borekitas in town. Or if you prefer, we can buy some and eat them at home."

"We'll go buy them and eat at home," he said.

"Okay," she said.

They walked to Leon's and chose some eggplant, cheese, and mushroom borekitas, with brown hard-boiled eggs to go with them. They went back home, Rey made coffee and brought out assorted cheese and olives, and they sat on the balcony and ate to their hearts' content. Israel took out of his bag a good bottle of wine and a small birthday present for Rey. "Happy birthday," he said, and he kissed her.

"Thank you," she said. "The real present is you coming to be with me today. I really appreciate it. This does not go without saying."

They sat and talked some more and then went up to the bedroom for their magic ritual. They stayed in bed and talked; it was something familiar, special, and intimate, totally theirs.

It was late afternoon, and Rey said, "I'm hungry. I planned for us to go down to that restaurant on the beach. They have good food there. What do you think? It's a beautiful day. I hope they have space available."

She called the place to book a table and was told it would be ready in forty-five minutes. She suggested that until then, they go for a walk on the beach. They went down to the beach. Rey tried to hold his hand to see how he reacted. He looked at her and said, "Stop it. You are embarrassing me."

"Why?" she asked.

"I have to refuse despite the fact that I really like that."

"Okay, relax," she said. "I just wanted to see your reaction."

"Okay," he said, a bit angry, "so now you know."

They went to the restaurant, and in a few moments, the hostess showed them to their table, which was right up front, facing the sea. *Great*, Rey thought, *and I didn't even ask for it.* "Thanks," she said to the waitress. "It's my birthday today."

"With pleasure," the hostess replied.

They sat down. The restaurant was packed.

"We were lucky," he said.

"We did the magic," Rey said happily.

The sun was warm and pleasant, and the blue sea was calm. Israel looked around, amazed at the restaurant, the view, and the people. He said, "Who needs to go overseas? Look at the beauty we have here."

"That's true," she said. "I love this place, especially due to its location and the view. And I almost always order the same thing: fried squid."

"I want that too," he said.

"Whatever you wish, darling. I suggest you order something else, and then we can share. How about that?"

"Yes, that's a great idea. Let's do that." He ordered meatballs with chilies and cold white wine with appetizers.

Israel seemed to be enjoying the moment, realizing there was life beyond the place where he lived. *Okay*, she thought, *he couldn't figure this out the day we met?* Then she said to herself, *You're being a bit patronizing.*

When they finished eating, the restaurant was nearly empty, and a gentle breeze was blowing, carrying the intoxicating smell of salty sea air, which reminded Rey of passionate memories from the past. When the sun was on its way to illuminate the other side of the planet, Rey said, "Shall we go?"

"Yes," he said, and they walked back to the apartment. He could not stop telling Rey how fascinated he was with everything—the restaurant, the sea, the view, the peaceful atmosphere. Even though Israel came almost every week, they'd never left the apartment, so he hadn't had an opportunity to see what was around.

She bought the weekend newspapers and some nuts, a ritual from long-gone days. When they arrived home, she said she was going to take a nap, and Israel said he would make some coffee and go over the newspapers. This was a weird situation for Rey; this was the time when Israel usually left on his way back, and she was left to herself and her thoughts and sweet memories of the day. *Well, we'll see how the next twenty-four hours unfold. That will be interesting.*

When she woke up, it took her a few moments to understand that Israel was sleeping next to her. She hadn't felt him come to bed. It was nice, and she lay there for a little while, pondering.

She got up and went downstairs for her ritual of lighting the Shabbat candles to express her gratitude for all of the good things of the past week and make her wishes for the coming week. She liked this ritual and tried to do it regularly. She did not hear Israel come down the stairs, and when she turned, she saw him standing there, smiling.

"You lit Shabbat candles?" he asked.

"Yes," she replied, "every Friday."

"Yes, we did that at my mom's house and do it in my house too."

He approached her and gave her a hug, and she whispered in his ear, "Shabbat shalom."

"And happy birthday," he added.

Rey started to set the table for dinner; they seemed to be constantly eating. *Well, it's not every day there are guests for a birthday dinner.*

It was nice. Rey enjoyed the festive atmosphere and having Israel over for Shabbat dinner. He offered to help and prepared the dressing for the salad. When they sat at the table, Rey asked if he would like to make a kiddush, a Friday night blessing over the wine.

"Not really," he said, "but let's have a toast. L'chaim."

They enjoyed good food and a pleasant atmosphere. It was nice and easy. They watched the news, talked politics a little, watched a movie, and went upstairs to the bedroom. Rey went to bed, switched on her bedside lamp, and took a book from the stand. A few moments later, Israel said, "It seems as if we have been married for twenty years."

"And what is wrong with that?" she asked. She looked at him, and he seemed to be offended, sulking. "What happened, darling?"

"What happened?" he said. "I am here in bed next to you, which is not a usual thing, and you are reading a book. That's nice. That's really nice."

"And why do you think I have to guess what your wishes are? Tell me what your wishes are, and your wish is my command. Your pleasure is my treasure. If you want something, my dear, please say it, or go for it."

Rey switched off the light, took off her pajamas, and crawled to him. *Men,* she thought, *are from Mars. Go figure.*

The Shabbat was peaceful. When they woke up, it was nearly ten o'clock. Israel said he did not remember when he'd slept that late. "Maybe the reason is that you are simply relaxed," she said.

"Yes," he said, "maybe."

Rey noticed that he was acting like a fish out of the water. *Well, the good is not obvious; you have to be ready to accept it and, more importantly, to believe you deserve it.*

"What would you like for breakfast?" she asked. "It's been some time since we last ate."

"Ha, I don't know," he replied. "I trust you will come up with something special. Tell me how I can help."

She decided on eggs Benedict. It was packed with taste and calories, but it was not something one ate every day. Once in a blue moon, it was okay.

Toward the afternoon hours, Rey noticed Israel becoming restless. She asked if everything was okay, he said yes, but she was not sure he was telling the truth.

Around three o'clock, he said he wanted to leave so he didn't get stuck in traffic. He packed his stuff, said it was fun, and kissed her lightly on her lips, and he was gone. Rey had a feeling something was wrong. Since breakfast, he'd been pensive and seemed to be elsewhere. She decided to let it be; he would share it with her when he was ready.

In his normal weekly visits, Israel used to call her from the road to tell her how much he enjoyed their time together and how fulfilling and meaningful their relationship was for him. He said it gave him strength until their next visit. This time, he did not call, nor did she receive an email from him the next morning, as she usually did. Rey decided not to call or write. His email arrived two days later:

Rey,

After I did quite a bit of thinking and reflecting on our weekend over and over again and after considering my ability to continue this relationship, I think it's best if we go our separate ways. I wish you all the best in whatever you do, and thanks for everything.

Quite like him, she said to herself. She already knew that was his way of dealing with challenges: simply not dealing with them. He suddenly had seen that there was another life out there and had realized that maybe it was time for him to do something about it, and he'd freaked out. The easiest thing for him to do was not to do anything and to stay in his muddy but familiar swamp. She decided not to react, at least for now.

What hurt her more than anything was the fact that he'd decided not to share his thoughts and difficulties with her. She was past the stage of weekly one-day hideaway meetings; for her, that was not enough anymore. Israel could not make the change in his approach to their relationship, and she knew that even if he did, it had to come from his own will and understanding that he needed to get out of the place he was in. It had to be something he personally wanted to do regardless of anything else. *Well, time will tell.*

CHAPTER

Nineteen

DURING THE NEXT FEW months, she turned the issue over and over in her mind. She sat with Ronen, and for hours, they talked about it. More than anything else for Rey was the process she herself was going through in her journey from emotional and physical wilderness to awakening, amazing discoveries she'd experienced, and who she had become. Maybe the emotional coma she'd been in during the fifteen years after Mike's death had been a reflection of her need for maturing to what she was now. Everything had changed, including herself.

They were out of touch for five months. One day she sent a message to all of the friends on her email list. Israel was on that list too. She realized it only after she got his answer.

Good morning.

Your words seem to break the barrier I worked so hard to build in trying to forget what we had together. I admit that frequently, especially on full moon nights like in the last few days, my thoughts wander to the beach and the ones living by.

Israel

Rey was moved by his words. His message reminded her of what they'd had, but she also noticed he did not offer anything. She knew that another email or two would bring them together again. She yearned for that togetherness, the emails, the phone conversations, and their being together.

Except for flirting here and there online, she did not meet anyone of interest. Rey was sure nothing had changed with Israel. He lived at home in his own private jail cell and was lonely. He had no one to share his thoughts, feelings, or sadness with, not a soul, but Rey could not help him as long as he refused to help himself. If she responded to his email in order to renew their relationship, she needed to understand that nothing had changed, and what had been was what would be. Israel, at that time, was not capable of giving her more. She decided to wait a week and see how she felt. If she still missed him and was ready to be satisfied with what he was able to offer her at that time, she would write to him.

A week went by. Rey sent him an email saying she'd had no conscious intention of contacting him, and it probably had been a Freudian slip. She asked how he was doing and said she missed him. Four days later, she got his reply:

> Good morning, woman of mine. There is nothing like beginning my day by reading words you write to me. It's like blessed rain on a scorched land. You have so much soul, and it is comforting to know that in the midst of all the hardship, there is a ray of abundance to

enjoy a moment. Happy you're here, happy I am here, and happy that we are (almost) together. From Me.

They got together again, and their renewed date was even more exciting than their first one. The peace lasted for a few months, when the old hardships popped again.

Rey knew that individuals sometimes met people in the course of their lives who came out of nowhere, gave them something they desperately needed at that time, and then vanished into thin air. They left simply because they had done what they'd come for. Rey decided to take time out.

She found a part-time job and enjoyed it. She, Batya, and their friend Ronit went out together to lectures, restaurants, and bars. Rey had them over and cooked. They ate, drank, laughed, and had a good time. There was nothing like the energy in women's camaraderie.

It seemed to Rey it was time to move on. She had passed the stage of flirting with young men. She'd gone through the journey of awakening, partying, and self-discovery, and now she had reached a crossroads. It was time to examine what she wanted and where she was heading. She knew exactly what type of men were suited for a long-term relationship. Rey was a strong woman with high self-awareness, inner strength, and the ability to adjust to anything she chose. She needed a strong man who was open-minded and had the ability to contain her and allow her the space she needed in order to have a good, healthy relationship. She also knew she could provide the same she was asking for. They had to have mutual things in common, of course, but different areas of interest as well to enable room to grow and private personal space. Rey knew that when the right man showed up, he probably would not be custom made for her; she would have to be flexible, make room for him, and learn that at times, they'd have to agree to disagree. As someone clever once had said, "If two people think the same, want the same, and do the same, one of them is obsolete."

She had no doubt that was what she wanted and could have. She was ready. Now she needed to wait for the opportunity. She freshened up her profile on the dating website, replaced her photographs, and changed her preferences, mainly the age of the men she was interested in. Sixty-five years old was still younger than she was but did not seem old to her anymore. *If I, at my age, look much younger and am energetic and young-spirited, there is no doubt in my mind there is a man suited for me somewhere on the planet. I just need to attract him to my life.*

She made her decision. Young men who approached her were deleted from her profile instantly; she was not even tempted to check them out. Men who claimed to be separated or had complex lives were out of the race too. She was after a simple relationship with no excess baggage or bitterness. She sought someone able and willing to create a mature, enjoyable relationship.

The first man she met was Michael. He was divorced, seventy years of age, and a retired sea captain. They talked a few times on the phone, and she agreed to meet him. She decided not to be prejudiced or judgmental. She'd never dated a man that old.

He asked where they should meet, and she gave him her address and asked him to please pick her up. He arrived on time, and they went to Jaffa. He said his daughter lived there, and he knew a few nice places where they could sit. It seemed Michael was a citizen of the world; he'd been to many places and had loads of stories and plenty of adventures. Rey loved those kinds of stories, and during the first times they met, she sat and listened, fascinated.

She later visited him at his home. He had a beautiful house in Haifa, with an amazing view of Mt. Carmel and Haifa Bay. The house looked as if it had not had a woman's touch for a long time. Michael liked good food and had an impressive collection of wines and alcoholic drinks. He liked her a lot, and soon enough, he asked her to move in with him.

"You will not have to work. I will take care of you," he said.

However, Rey felt he was looking for a companion, a kind of upgraded kept woman. She noticed he did not ask anything about her life—he seemed to have no interest. If she initiated a conversation on the subject, he interrupted her because that reminded him of something. She knew Michael was not the one.

Next was Daniel, a sixty-three-year-old divorcé from Tel Aviv who dealt with antiques. *That's good*, she thought. As Agatha Christie, whose husband was an archeologist, had said, "The older I get, the more interesting to him." Daniel had long gray hair tied in a kind of ponytail—Rey loved men with long hair; she thought it was sexy—and he loved jazz. Their first date was good. They sat in a café, had a vibrant conversation, and laughed a lot. When he drove her back home, he said he'd had a lot of fun. "You should have warned me," he added.

"Why?" she asked.

"You are very cute."

He said he wanted to see her again, and she replied, "That would be nice."

She called him a few times. Once, he was in a business meeting and said he would call her back. He called her twenty-four hours later. It was a Thursday. She asked if he would like to meet on Friday in the late morning for coffee.

"No," he said. "Friday I hang out with my daughter who lives with me."

"So when is a good time?" she asked.

"I'll call you later, and we'll decide."

Okay, she thought. *I get it. Everything at the last minute. If that is his only fault, I can live with that.*

It was almost six o'clock Friday evening, Shabbat, and she still had not heard from Daniel. She decided not to call him. Finally, he called. "Hi, sweetie. What's up?" he asked.

"I'm fine, and you?"

"I thought I would come over to your place at about seven thirty or eight."

"Come to my place?" Rey asked.

Daniel didn't answer at first and then said, "Well, I don't know."

"Daniel," Rey said, "if you are coming to my house on Friday evening at eight o'clock, that means you coming for a Shabbat dinner, and I have not prepared anything."

"Oh," he said. "Okay, if you want to go out for dinner, just say it."

Rey wanted to tell him to go to hell and hang up on him, but she didn't. Instead, she said, "Is that your usual way of inviting a woman out for dinner?"

Daniel understood he'd screwed up and said, "No, not really. I know it came out crooked. I'm sorry. I had a hard day. My daughter drives me crazy, and I just was not thinking straight."

"You are forgiven this time," she said.

"Okay, I'll pick you up around eight. I'll call from downstairs."

"Okay," she replied, and she hung up. The truth was, she did not feel like meeting Daniel or having dinner with him.

A good sandwich with a glass of wine at home is much more tempting, but okay, let it be.

Rey was losing her patience with Daniel. It was impossible to make any plans with him, and when they met, he talked nonstop and "helped" her finish her sentences because he already knew what she wanted to say. He also made fun of everything. She tried to check with herself if she was being too judgmental or if this relationship was not it. She asked herself if she enjoyed his company, looked forward to meeting him, and was attracted to him physically, and after she met with him a few times, the answer was no. *Okay, then so be it.* She saw this as another part of her journey. Until now, she'd met with young men. The purpose had been different, and so had the energy

Now she was seeing older men. Many had traveled parts of their journeys with other mates and had families, and all of that was a part of their lives she did not belong to—same as with her life. It was kind of a package deal. Rey knew exactly what she was looking for: a partner to continue the journey—someone who would be a friend, a lover, and a confidant, in that order. Those qualities were a must.

Rey had spent a long time on her own and knew the advantages of single life. She liked having company and being with people, but she also liked the solitary life, especially the peace and the freedom to come and go as she pleased and do whatever she liked without having to answer to anyone. She used to say jokingly that she and Rey got along perfectly together, and in order to let someone in, they had to make room. Her high level of consciousness helped her identify the challenges arising from time to time and deal with them. Despite all of the work she did, the challenges did not disappear completely, but the ability to catch them in real time helped her, and they happened less often. One of them was the issue of her chronological age. She felt she was racing against time and feared she might not manage to do everything she wanted. She knew she looked great; people told her over and over that she looked a lot younger than her age, but the fear of old age crept in every now and then—the fear she would be considered old and be old, needy, and weak. Those words raised enormous fear in her; they were synonyms for a loss of control, betrayal of the body, weakness of the brain, dependency, and inability to control her life. *But what is the meaning of being young? How does that express itself? Is it the way you look? Smooth skin? A well-shaped body? Toned muscles? Erect breasts? To be cool, to have erotic thoughts, to feel sexual desire, or to have multiple orgasms? Have physical strength? Or maybe the constant desire to learn, try new things, get excited, laugh a lot, be amazed like a child, and have a spark in your eyes. Maybe it's the knowledge that there is nothing I want that I cannot experience. Maybe it's to find the peace within, the feeling that the sky is the limit, and also to learn to love yourself and accept yourself the way you are now unconditionally—no ifs, ands, or buts.*

Rey was healthy in body and soul, and despite the fact that young people got sick too, the words *old age* had a terrifying and threatening sound to her. There were days when, in every TV program she watched and every book she read, she saw only the young, the ones the world belonged to. Their whole lives were ahead of them. She felt a flood of adrenaline, strength, and energy wanting to burst out, and in that moment, she did not know how to handle that, what to do, or how to channel the energy. Should she take a sports car driving course? Should she get into the driver's seat and step on the gas until the speedometer needle hit bottom and she felt that she and the car were one? Or to do a free-fall skydiving jump into the blue horizon, into the unknown, the divine, and enjoy the feeling of ultimate freedom while gliding, floating in the air, and screaming, "Born to be alive!"?

She had a need to really feel she was alive. The next question that came was *Do you have to do something extreme to really feel alive? Maybe to feel alive is to find a place inside and have the knowledge that I am safe because the sense of security comes from within me, and wherever I go, I take myself with me. Whatever happens, I always have me to count on.*

Rey was in a sort of dating marathon; she checked all of the dating websites and took the time and energy to find a mate. She dated a lot, going out with men mostly once or twice. In order not to exhaust herself, she had to better screen the candidates as well as trust her instincts. It happened sometimes that she thought someone was not suitable, but then she checked with herself to see if she was being too quick to judge, so she dated him anyway. One of those was Oudi.

Oudi approached her on one of the dating websites. He wrote that he would like to talk to her. He was divorced, was sixty-eight, and lived in the area. His photograph was reasonable. She sent him her phone number, and he called two days later. They talked, and he said he did not like long phone conversations; if there was an interest, they should meet and carry on the conversation in person. That phone conversation lasted about an hour, and Rey said they would talk again.

He called again at ten o'clock that night and said, "I thought you said you would call."

"Yes," Rey replied, "I meant tomorrow."

For one who does not like phone conversations, he's not doing too bad, she thought.

"Look," he said, "I have reception problems in my house, so I left the house, and I am on the street now so I can talk to you uninterrupted."

Wow, she thought.

They talked until one o'clock in the morning. He told her he was divorced, had one daughter, and had studied in the USA. She didn't quite understand what he'd studied and what his occupation was. He said he liked photography and was retired.

"So what are you doing with yourself?" she asked.

He did not reply. In his profile, he'd mentioned he was a smoker, so she asked him if he smoked much. He said, "I don't like people counting my money or the number of cigarettes I smoke."

She had a feeling he was testing her, and it was okay with her. Rey's ego had been in its proper place for a long time now, so she disregarded the tone and content of his reply and went along with it.

He called again the next morning and said he really wanted to see her. They decided to meet at a place by the beach. Rey recognized him from the picture in his profile. He was a big guy wearing sloppy-looking clothes and a backpack. They sat down in a small café and ordered. He took out a pack of cigarettes and lit one. Rey noticed he did not ask her if it would bother her, and then he said something interesting: "I was thinking about how I can charm you so that you can see beyond my smoking and my belly."

They sat for six long hours. Oudi talked most of the time, and Rey listened. Cold wind started blowing, and Rey said she needed to go. He walked with her for a while and said he thought they were so good together that it would be a disaster if they missed that opportunity. Before they parted, he asked, "What are you doing tonight?"

She said, "Nothing special."

"So can I come over?"

"No," Rey said without hesitation. "I want to go home now to have a warm shower. I am freezing. Then I will eat something and do work on my computer."

"Okay," he said, and they parted.

They met again the next day. He picked her up, and they sat in a café at the park. It was pretty much the same ritual: he talked constantly, and he corrected her grammatical mistakes when she had a chance to say something. He named authors and historic events. She noticed he was sitting too close for comfort, just as he had on their first date, and he was very enthusiastic. *About what?* she wondered. She could not think straight about how she felt about this. *Too much. Too intense.* She felt she couldn't breathe.

This date too lasted for a few hours. Again, it was Rey who said she needed to go. He took her home, Rey thanked him, and he said he wanted to come up. It was the same thing again. *What is it with this guy? He does not know when to stop!* He insisted he wanted to come up. With all of the embarrassment she felt, she wanted to be alone now, and that was what she told him. "I have the need to be with myself now," she said.

"And what about my need?" he asked.

She did not know what to say and was silent. She could not understand the pressure he was putting on her, and she resented it. Finally, she said, "Thanks. Bye-bye," and she got out of the car.

She called him later that evening and said she'd felt uncomfortable with the way they'd parted and asked if she'd offended him. He said yes, he was hurt. Rey apologized and said that had not been her intention.

"Maybe you should have thought about it before you said it," he replied.

There was a moment of silence, and then Rey said, "Okay, have a pleasant evening." He hung up.

The next day, she did not hear from him and decided to call. When he answered the phone, she asked him if he would like to meet, and he said, "I'm not sure if I want to."

"Would you like to explain?" she asked, and he said no. Rey wished him a nice day and hung up.

The event made Rey rethink the whole thing. Oudi was somewhat obsessive, but what could she learn from it? Her conclusion was that she needed to stop to reexamine all of the red lights blinking along the way and maybe look at her obsessive need for freedom. She would have to learn to make room and share her private space if she really wanted to create a relationship. One thing she knew for sure was that Oudi was definitely not the one. She decided to take time out again to release the stress, and when the time was right, the right guy would show up.

The interesting thing was the metamorphosis Rey had gone through in her journey. She'd discovered in herself something she had not known existed. A hidden reservoir of energy and strength had emerged and given her an amazing sense of freedom. She felt as if she were on an infinite runway, waiting to take off.

Epilogue

Rey was one of those who liked stories with happy endings. "Our life is stressful enough," she would say, "and has sadness and disappointments, so at least stories should have happy endings."

So did Rey's story have a happy ending? That depended on what the definition of a happy ending was. A happy ending, in Rey's case, could be finding a mate after her heart or perhaps coming to the conclusion that she was responsible for her own happiness and was entitled to decide, as a single woman, what type of relationship she was looking for at that time. Perhaps a happy ending for Rey lay in the fact that she discovered she had other sides to her she'd never known existed. She allowed them to surface and reveal themselves, which brought a sense of freedom and peace. In peace and tranquility, fear, doubt, and confusion evaporated, and clarity emerged.

Maybe her happy ending included all of the above. The answer is for the reader to decide. Rey's story is about the reality that everything is possible at any time. In one of her workshops, Batya said, "Our personality is like a string of pearls. Each pearl represents a part of the personality, and all of them create the whole string of pearls."

In each of us exists the woman, friend, mother, wife, lover, daughter, queen, maid, and, as Pinkola Estes wrote, *vieja que sabe* (old woman who knows), the wild woman.

Rey's story is the story of women who reach their golden age and find themselves single again yet still have strong passion for life, vitality, and plenty of energy to look for the kind of relationship suitable for them at the time.

Modern society seems to leave this issue underneath the surface with no real legitimacy and even promote a hidden message that it is somewhat pathetic to seek a relationship at such an age.

Well, Rey has news for you: it is possible, advised, and even desirable at any age if you wish. Love, excitement, and sex are not just for the young. Even in senior years, people can experience strong, powerful passion for life.

I wrote this book because I wanted to share with readers my exceptional journey from the time I lost my husband until I came back to the land of the living, so to speak, as a woman, allowing myself to live life to the fullest in all aspects. This book is not about sex, fame, or money. This book is about a phenomenon. For many years, I had a war of attrition with my chronological age, my age as it appears on my ID card—my date of birth. To me, this chronological age meant I was old, and that was a dirty word. To me, old age meant disease, disability, and betrayal of the body. It meant not being considered; having a lower self-image; and being at the bottom of the food chain for jobs, dating, and more. I resented it, and it scared me to death. I always looked younger—people told me that. The wonder was that I slowly I realized that as I grew older, my mental body grew younger. The levels of energy were unbelievable.

Now, if I have the blues, I listen to music on my Shazam application, from Bonny M. to Gloria Gaynor to George Michael, and in a split second, the beat of the music changes my frequency and vibration. I find myself hopping all over the place. I have all kinds of ideas running through my head. I'm curious about things I want to know and learn. When I talk about things I want to do, I get rosy cheeks, my eyes shine, and I get everybody around me excited. I want to write books, travel the world, go to Vietnam and Cambodia, sail on the Mekong River, visit the monasteries, go on culinary trips, learn to cook exotic foods, take a trip in the desert with nomads on camels so I can have firsthand experience for one of the books I am planning to write, do volunteer work with children, and more. When I look in the mirror, I see a young woman wanting to conquer the world. I know there is nothing I can't do once I put my mind to it.

Slowly but surely, my physical body has started following my mental body. Little ailments have disappeared. I went to renew my driver's license and was told I don't need glasses anymore. My physical strength and flexibility have improved. I sleep eight to nine hours a night, and I am not using any medication except for a hormone replacement that keeps me sexually able and willing. People think I am fifteen to twenty years younger than my chronological age. I am seventy-seven, but I look sixty, and I feel like a thirty-five-year-old single woman with her whole life ahead of her.

I am sharing this with you because it is my doing. I started a process and followed my intuition—my gut feeling. Some was intentional, and some was subconscious. I love every minute of this journey. I wake up in the morning with a song playing in my head: "I'm gonna live forever. I'm gonna learn how to fly high." For me, this is my second time around without having to die first. This is my calling, and I want to reveal it to you. But beware: it might be contagious.

Printed in the United States
By Bookmasters